PERIL AT THE WORLD'S BIGGEST HOCKEY TOURNAMENT

Roy MacGregor

McClelland & Stewart

For my young cousins, Simon and Kieran Day, future hockey stars, current terrific kids.

Library and Archives Canada Cataloguing in Publication

MacGregor, Roy, 1948–
    Peril at the world's biggest hockey tournament / Roy MacGregor.

(The Screech Owls series ; #21)
ISBN 978-0-7710-5607-9

    I. Title. II. Series.

PS8575.G84P47 2008   jC813'.54   C2007-906404-3

We acknowledge the financial support of the Government of Canada through the Book Publishing Industry Development Program and that of the Government of Ontario through the Ontario Media Development Corporation's Ontario Book Initiative. We further acknowledge the support of the Canada Council for the Arts and the Ontario Arts Council for our publishing program.

Typeset in Bembo by M&S, Toronto

McClelland & Stewart Ltd.
75 Sherbourne Street
Toronto, Ontario
M5A 2P9
www.mcclelland.com

1 2 3 4 5   12 11 10 09 08

You can call me Al.

But you can also call me
Claude, or Charlie, or Tarek, or
Sanchez, or Vladimir, or
Muhammad, or Yin, or
Talwinder — or, for that matter,
Suzy, Shazia, Sabrina . . .

i am none of these people. i am
all of these people. i am what
lies, waiting, underneath your
bed at night. i am what lurks
around the next corner.
i am what you fear when a
news flash interrupts regular
programming on your television.
i am what you dread when your
phone rings late at night with a
long-distance call.

i am the darkness that is so
complete, there will never be light
again.

This is my diary.

And you are now part of it,
whether you wish to be or not.

My plan is to mail this diary on
the Day of Reckoning. it is not
to let people know who i am, or
who i was. it is important that no
one ever knows my identity so
that many are blamed for what
will happen in Ottawa, Canada,
on January 1.

1/1. The first day of the year.
The last day for so many.

i want to see the blame spread
wide and far. i want no one to
know exactly who is guilty so
that all will be under suspicion.

i want children to fear the one
they love.

And i want them to know how i did it, how stunningly simple it was for one man (or woman, for all you will ever know) to accomplish what a dozen hijacked airplanes could never manage.

All for the cost of a hot dog.

And this, my diary, will serve as a faithful record of what went wrong.

So brilliantly, easily wrong.

TRAVIS WAS LOSING CONSCIOUSNESS.

First, he could feel the hands, then the thick arms, wrapping around his neck and tightening, hard. Then he was on the floor, kicking, struggling, trying to figure out how it could have come to this.

He was being strangled by his very best friend in the world, Wayne Nishikawa.

Travis could smell Nish's stale sweat. The only smell worse than this, in his experience, had come from a skunk his father squashed while driving through the fog to get to his grandparents' cottage. He could feel fresher sweat, slippery and warm on his face, the salt stinging his eye, as one of Nish's fat arms slid up and over his mouth and nose while the other held fast, tightening still, around his throat.

Travis was blacking out.

"All right, you two – break it up!"

The voice came from somewhere far away. From heaven? No, it was too close for that, and besides,

Travis wasn't dead; he could feel himself still breathing, if only barely.

It was the commanding voice of Mr. Dillinger, the Screech Owls' team manager.

"*Break it up! You hear me, Nish?*"

Travis could feel Mr. Dillinger's big hairy hands on him now. They were prying away the slippery, sweaty arms of Travis's best friend and attempted murderer.

Travis broke free and rolled over onto his back, staring up. Mr. Dillinger, the ring of hair around his bald head standing out over his ears like a clown, had grabbed Nish's stinking T-shirt in both hands and lifted him clear off the ground. Nish's arms and legs flailed helplessly, as if Mr. Dillinger had plucked up a crayfish before it could slip back under a rock.

Travis might have laughed if he weren't close to dying. He gasped for breath. His eyes were wet and stinging, and when he looked around, his teammates seemed distorted and watery, almost as if he were looking at their reflections in a funhouse mirror.

Sarah Cuthbertson and Sam Bennett were holding onto each other as if the two girls had just witnessed something horrible, like a car accident . . . or a murder. Data was in his wheelchair by the door – he must have been the one who called Mr. Dillinger in from the skate-sharpening machine to stop the fight. The rest were standing around, staring in shock at the scene on the dressing room floor: little Simon Milliken, his eyes so wide they seemed larger than his glasses; Jenny Staples and Jeremy Weathers, half-dressed in their goaltending equipment; Derek Dillinger, Gordie Griffith, Wilson Kelly, Andy Higgins, Jesse Highboy, Dmitri Yakushev, and Willie Granger, all looking sheepish, as if they should have done something to prevent Nish's attack on Travis, their team captain.

Fahd Noorizadeh and Lars Johanssen were laughing — almost as if they thought Nish had been putting on another of his fake wrestling "shows" to get everyone's attention.

But this had been real. Almost *too* real. And it had all started so innocently.

2

"WE *HAVE* TO DO THIS!"

It was six months before Nish's attempted murder of his best friend in the world. Willie Granger was speaking in the Owls' dressing room, and he was insistent.

It was rare for Willie to get so wound up. He was usually the quiet one, the stay-at-home defenceman who did such odd things as *read* on the team bus. According to Nish, there should be a misconduct penalty for anyone carrying books to a tournament.

Willie himself should have been in *The Guinness Book of World Records* for the number of records he knew off the top of his head – with a particular love of the truly gross ones.

Want to know who has the world's longest finger-nails? Just ask Willie. "Lee Redmond, Utah – total nail length, approximately the distance between the blue line and the red line in a North American hockey rink."

The world record for body piercing? "Elaine Davidson, Scotland – 720 piercings, including 192 on her face alone."

The largest dew worm ever found? "Africa – 54.86 metres long, roughly the distance from net to net."

The longest fart ever recorded? "Bernard Clemmens, London, England – two minutes and forty-two seconds of continuous sound.

"*However,*" Willie was quick to add, "this remarkable feat has never been verified by *The Guinness Book of World Records* – the only authority on world records I accept. Besides, anyone who has ever played for the Screech Owls knows Nish beats that so-called record every bus trip!"

But this time, Willie, the endless researcher, had found something new: a reference in the newspaper to the Bell Capital Cup, a peewee hockey tournament in Ottawa that was claiming to be bigger than any other in the world. This year, the organizers had got the Guinness officials to come to officially declare the event the World's Biggest Hockey Tournament. Some five hundred teams were expected to attend, and according to one newspaper report, teams were coming from Russia, Finland, Sweden, Denmark, Switzerland, England, Australia, Japan, China, Kazakhstan, the United States, Mexico, and, of course, from all over Canada.

"We *have* to go!" Willie repeated.

It didn't take much to convince the team. It took considerable effort, however, to sell coach Muck Munro on the idea.

Muck believed the holiday season was for family, not hockey tournaments. He didn't even like to schedule practices around the New Year. He always said there should be a time during every hockey season when everyone just forgot about the game for a little bit. Do something different, he would tell them. Go skiing. Go skate with your family on an outdoor rink. Read a book (a suggestion that always made Nish grab his throat as if he was about to throw up).

"We can have our outdoor skate in Ottawa," Willie argued. "The Rideau Canal is the world's longest skating rink. My *Guinness Book of World Records* says it's 7.8 kilometres, one end to the other. We could skate there as a team."

Muck wasn't convinced.

It was Sarah who came up with the clincher. She suggested they could do something educational in Ottawa, like visit the National Gallery of Canada, or the Museum of Civilization, or – and here she glanced quickly at Travis – the new War Museum.

Travis almost giggled out loud. He knew exactly what Sarah was up to. Muck was a strange man. He had spent his life in hockey – all the older people in

Tamarack said he once was a shoo-in to make the NHL, right up until he had that awful leg injury – and you might expect him to spend his evenings watching hockey games on television. But that wasn't Muck. His hobby was history books, particularly books about the two world wars, and the only time he ever bothered to turn on his old black-and-white television was for the history channel.

If anyone could change Muck's mind, it would be Sarah, the pony-tailed centre everyone said was a future Olympian.

"Too expensive," he argued, but you could tell he was bending.

"We'll do bottle drives," Sam countered.

"Instead of getting us Christmas presents," Gordie Griffith suggested, "we'll ask our parents to sponsor us."

"I'm off work that week," Mr. Dillinger offered. "If we use the old bus, we'll save on gas."

It was obvious Mr. Dillinger really wanted to go. He was nervously tugging at his thick black moustache as he waited for Muck's response.

"What about your schooling?" Muck asked the Screech Owls. "You'll have assignments over the break."

"We'll take them with us," Lars said. "We can do them on the bus – and in the hotel."

This was a bit much for Nish. "Count me out!" he shouted. "I thought you said it was a hockey tournament we were going to – not a *prison!*"

"Don't be stupid!" Sam snapped, then smiled sadly at Nish. "Ohhh, sorry. I forgot, it's impossible for you to be anything but!"

Nish blew a raspberry at her.

Muck said he'd need a day to think about it. What he was really doing, Travis knew, was taking some time to ask the Owls' parents. Muck would call them all first. If there was one family who felt they couldn't afford it, he might still go and play a player short, but if two or more families couldn't manage it, he'd squash the suggestion before it went any further.

Travis was in bed re-reading Harry Potter when the call came in to the Lindsay house. He could hear his father talking to Muck about the big trade the Maple Leafs had just made with the Colorado Avalanche, and then the talk turned to hotels, which Travis took to be a good sign.

"There's a big political gathering in Ottawa that week," Mr. Lindsay was saying. "All the major trading nations will be there – it's Canada's turn to host."

His dad went quiet for a moment while he listened to whatever Muck was saying.

"Well," he said, finally, "I'd grab it if I were you.

Rooms are going to be hard to come by because of that conference. . . . I know it's more than we're used to paying, but it's holiday rates, you have to expect to pay a premium. . . . I see. . . . Sounds good to us. Count Travis in."

That was all Travis needed to hear. He closed his book and turned out the light. He was asleep almost before the room was dark.

He knew what he'd be dreaming about tonight: taking to the ice at Scotiabank Place with Sarah and Nish and all the other Owls, skating and scoring and starring, in their own smaller way, on the same ice surface where Ottawa Senators like Daniel Alfredsson and Dany Heatley and Jason Spezza had played. A real NHL rink, where visiting teams included players like Sidney Crosby, Alexander Ovechkin, the Staal brothers, Jaromir Jagr, and, once upon a time, Mario Lemieux. The rink where Wayne Gretzky announced his retirement and played his final game in Canada.

How could Travis know that this one small fact about Wayne Gretzky would cause his very best friend in the entire world to try to kill him?

December 15

Al here again,

if you're wondering what i
look like, try the mirror. i'm in
there, somewhere. i promise you.

Look into your own eyes and
tell me, honestly, if you don't
see something very dark back
there, something hidden from
everyone in the world but
yourself, and possibly not
even recognized or acknowledged
by you, because it's just too
dark to deal with.

You think i wasn't a nice polite
kid myself once? i was. i went
to school and played sports and

used to dream about being a doctor. i'm very bright, you see.

And you WILL see — and SOON!

They called me "brilliant" when i was younger. But that was before i got smart. i got smart on a Tuesday morning around 8:46 A.M., Eastern Standard Time.

Perhaps you remember the day. Maybe you're too young. But everyone who was there — and "there," in this case, covers the entire world — remembers it as vividly as if it happened yesterday.

They call it 9/11.

i said earlier, you could call me Al — it's not my real name, you will never know that — but you can also call me 1/1.

The first day of the first month.

15

The first and last day of forever.

Time for me to drop a few hints, i think. Not that anyone will ever pick them up, since no one sees this diary but me — for the time being.

But i want to tell you a couple of things for when the so-called "experts" are looking back, trying to piece together what happened on the day that will be forever remembered as 7/7 — My Day, Your Day, O-Day.

"O" stands for Ottawa. i'm here now. i have been here for some time. Maybe years. Maybe months. You will never know. But believe me, i've been here long enough to set the plan in motion.

Ottawa, then. You can know that.

And you can know one other thing, as well. Even if you knew exactly what i looked like, you could be looking right at me and not see me at all.

You would see someone else.

And when you saw me, you would smile.

Think about it.

See if you can guess.

THE SCREECH OWLS HELD BOTTLE DRIVES AND collected tabs off pop cans and even tried something new – collecting and selling scrap metal. Eventually, they had raised enough money to cover the entry fee for the Bell Capital Cup.

The Owls left the day after Christmas, on Boxing Day. Mr. Dillinger, wearing a "Team Canada" toque perched on top of his bald spot, drove the team bus slowly up through Algonquin Park over snow-covered, often icy, roads. He had the heater on full blast, which meant that those in the front were too hot, while those in the back kept calling out that they were *"freezing* to death."

Muck paid no attention. He was reading some brick-thick history book in his reserved spot at the very front of the old bus: first seat, passenger side. "Riding shotgun," Muck called it.

"What's *shotgun?*" Fahd asked.

"The guy who used to sit beside the stagecoach driver always carried a shotgun in case of holdups," Muck patiently explained. "Ever since, they've called that seat the 'shotgun' seat."

Fahd looked hard at Muck. "How old *are* you, anyway?"

"Old enough to know better than you," Muck said. And that was the end of the discussion.

Sarah and Sam sat together, deep in their homework. Sam played with her thick carrot-red hair as she worked on math questions. Fahd, with his hood up for warmth, played with his Game Boy; Willie, wearing his Owls baseball cap backwards, studied his books of records and statistics; and most of the others quietly read books they'd been assigned by their teachers.

Nish farted.

Well, in truth, he didn't really fart. What he did was play fart tricks. He had a whoopee cushion, which he slipped onto Mr. Dillinger's seat just before he sat down at the start of the trip. And he had a bottle of "Flarp Noise Putty," which he'd picked up at Mr. Dillinger's traditional Stupid Stop, where each player had permission to spend up to five dollars on anything he or she liked.

Sam had bought an Archie and Veronica digest. Travis and some of the others bought packs of hockey cards. Jenny bought a toque that said "Canada" on it, which she was now wearing pulled down over her ears. And Nish? Nish bought farting putty. You poked your finger into a thick, jelly-like substance, and when you pulled it out, it made a huge sucking sound. Whenever the opportunity presented itself, Nish would lean down by a sleeping Owl, stick his finger into the jar, and then rip it out fast, making a farting sound so loud it would wake the sleeper – at which point Nish would grab his nose and pretend to faint.

"You're supposed to be studying, Nishikawa," Mr. Dillinger warned during a brief stop in Barry's Bay for them to stretch their legs and find a washroom.

"Exactly what I'm doing, sir," Nish answered with his most angelic look.

"Studying what?" Mr. Dillinger asked.

"For my post-playing days. I'll play ten or twelve years in the NHL, then take my act to Las Vegas."

"You think people will *pay* you to act like an idiot?" Jeremy shouted from the back of the lineup for the toilet.

"Maybe they'll pay him *not* to!" Sam shot back from the door to the girls' washroom.

"He'll make a fortune!" giggled Lars.

• • •

They arrived in Ottawa in a snowstorm, the wet snow sticking to the windshield wipers and the old bus slipping on the roads. For most of the journey, Mr. Dillinger had been anxiously running his hands through his sparse hair as he drove, and now tufts of it were standing up on both sides. He was visibly relieved they had made it through such awful conditions without the usual flat tire or breakdown, and everyone was glad to get out and booked into the hotel.

They were lucky to get lodging so close to the rink, Mr. Dillinger said. The big downtown hotels were taken up by politicians from all around the world. And there were more than five hundred peewee hockey teams in town, all needing rooms.

"You couldn't get a room in this city for a million bucks, now," Mr. Dillinger said as they lined up to register. "You kids want to thank your lucky stars you're in."

As usual, Travis would be rooming with Nish, as well as Lars and Fahd. It was a nice hotel near the main highway, with halls wide and long enough for a full-scale mini-sticks tournament. There was a small restaurant with inexpensive food. And, fortunately, there was *not* a water slide for Nish to dump a box of detergent into.

Muck wanted the Owls on the ice for their practice session as quickly as possible so the players could "find their legs."

"Mine are right where I put them this morning," Nish wisecracked, *"in my shoes!"*

"What you need is practice finding your brain," shot back Sam.

With Mr. Dillinger already warming up the bus again, the Owls were off to the rink.

THE SCREECH OWLS WERE ASSIGNED TO THE visitors' dressing room at Scotiabank Place. Each arriving team would have one practice session before their first game, but most teams were spread across the city in a dozen other rinks that would also be hosting the Bell Capital Cup. The six teams that got to practice at the big NHL rink were chosen by lottery, and by pure luck the Owls were one of them.

"Makes perfect sense," Nish said as he carried his equipment past the Zamboni chute to the dressing room. "May as well get a feel for the ice I'll be accepting the MVP award on – with appropriate fake humility, of course."

The tournament would last all week, with the final to be played at Scotiabank Place on New Year's Day. The year before, more than fifteen thousand fans had come out to watch the championship game, and this year the total was predicted to reach as high as twenty thousand – the same number that turned out to watch the Senators when they reached the Stanley Cup finals.

"We have to *get* there first," cautioned Travis. "There are some great teams here."

Travis had seen the list. Some of the teams were familiar to him. The Portland Panthers were here with Jeremy Billings and Stu Yantha, and Slava Shadrin's team was coming from Russia.

Travis had run a finger down the long list of teams. He recognized some of them from past tournaments, but most of them he didn't. He felt a shiver go up and down his spine. There was nothing more exciting, he thought, than taking to the ice against a team you had never seen before, never even heard of. How, he wondered, would the Screech Owls do against the Kazakhstan Komets? According to Muck, Kazakhstan was part of the old Soviet Union, a place so far away from Moscow it seemed more in China than Russia. The "Kaz" kids, Muck said, were being instructed by retired Russian players from the 1970s and 1980s, some of whom had actually played in the 1972 Summit Series. The Owls all knew about that historic hockey series. After all, it had been Muck's old pal and former junior teammate, Paul Henderson, who had scored the winning goal and given Canada the victory. Many said it was the greatest goal in the history of hockey.

"They play the old Russian style," Muck said with a chuckle. "I hope you kids get a chance to see it, because there's more than one way to play this game."

The visitors' dressing room in Scotiabank Place was unlike anything the Owls had seen before. It was an NHL dressing room, not the little cubby-hole they had to make do with at the far end of the Tamarack rink. It was huge. There was a table in the centre stacked with tapes of various colours – even the pink that Sarah favoured for her stick – and rooms off to the side for the trainers to ice players' injuries. There was an enormous washroom with eight separate showers. And in a corner was a full container of Gatorade with disposable cups already laid out for the Owls to drink as much as they wanted.

But there was another difference. The Owls were used to the layout of their own dressing room back in Tamarack, where all season long, they sat in exactly the same seats. Travis was pretty much in the centre, but not quite. The absolutely dead-centre seat in the Tamarack dressing room belonged to Nish, who claimed that, as assistant captain, he had to sit next to Travis. But Travis figured there was another reason. Nish wanted the centre spot so he could see Mr. Dillinger or Muck coming in and stop whatever hijincks he was up to, such as filling Travis's skates with Muck's shaving cream or cutting Fahd's skate laces in half.

Here, at Scotiabank Place, the visitors' dressing room was laid out differently, and the team's usual seating order was thrown off by the room's design. Everyone had to just grab a seat and forget about where they usually sat.

Travis's new seat was the very last locker on the right-hand side of the room. No big deal, he thought.

Nish took the first seat along the next wall. He seemed miffed. He dumped out his skunky equipment bag as if he were emptying a bucket of slop in a pigpen. When he'd finished shaking out his disgusting equipment, he sat down dramatically, arms folded high on his chubby chest, face ripening into that familiar tomato look that told everyone to steer clear.

"Hey, cool!" Simon said from the far side of the room. "Real hockey lockers – look at this!" Simon had lifted up the seat on his locker to reveal a storage area underneath.

Others picked up their seats, all of them impressed. This was a *real* NHL rink. These were *real* lockers, used by *real* NHL stars.

Travis turned up his seat. There was something hand-written on the underside. Someone had taken a thick black Sharpie pen and very carefully written out the following message:"Wayne Gretzky sat in this stall during his final game in Canada, April 15, 1999."

"What the . . . ?"

Jeremy leaned over to look. "Oh my God! *Wayne Gretzky* sat here!"

Screaming and yelling, the Owls descended on Travis's open locker. Some, like Sarah, stared open-mouthed, unable to say anything. Willie, the trivia nut, seemed close to tears. Lars was slapping Travis's back as if he'd just scored the biggest goal of a tournament.

"It's MY seat!" a voice thundered.

The excited chatter stopped, and everyone turned, as one, to stare at a fat face that looked about to burst.

Nish was furious.

"MY seat!" roared Nish. "Trav should be one seat over, and I sit next to him — *always.*"

"Grow up!" Sam snapped and turned back to admire the famous seat.

"Besides," Nish whined, "I'm the only one named Wayne. *I* should be there, not some guy named *Travis.*" He made the name sound like it was the most insulting word ever uttered.

Sarah started the laughter, and Simon and Lars were quick to join in. Then all the Screech Owls were laughing.

They weren't laughing at the way Nish said Travis's name — they were laughing at Nish for being such a baby.

And it was this precise moment that Nish turned into a madman.

He tackled the much-smaller Travis from behind, taking him to the floor as the Wayne Gretzky seat crashed back down.

Travis felt the thick arm of his best friend in the world snake around his neck and tighten.

December 27

Me again.

All goes according to plan. i
landed exactly the fake job i need
to get the real job done. The
fools won't even check out the
phony resume i handed in. They
never do. i come across so
convincing, so honest, so
trustworthy, i never get checked
out. Works every time.

Humans are stupid. i don't
consider myself one. Some
will call me sub-human once
this is all over, but i prefer
super-human. Something far
above the rot that politicians
have turned this world into.

i will be doing the world a favour. But no one will see it that way for a long, long time. You have to be super-human to see that far into the future, to know what needs to be done today so that there will be a tomorrow.

Mark it down: 7/7. They will say it was the day the world ended. But it will really be the day the new world began.

History will prove me right. Just you wait and see.

Am i bothering you yet?

i do hope so.

But, when you're thinking of me, you're not even close to seeing who i am or, for that matter, WHAT i am. i'm really quite warm and fuzzy.

That's me — warm and fuzzy all over.

TRAVIS WONDERED IF HE'D HAVE TO WEAR HIS neck guard for the rest of his life — or for at least as long as he and Nish remained friends.

Mind you, after Nish's outburst over a stupid seat in the dressing room, it was hard to think of him as any sort of friend.

Mr. Dillinger said they'd settle the seat situation out on the ice, during practice. He wouldn't say how, but it did get everyone concentrating once more on getting ready for the tournament. The Owls needed to get their focus back. They'd been off skates for nearly a week, now, and it was starting to show.

Stepping out onto the ice felt strange to Travis. It felt as if he had ski boots on, not skates. It always surprised Travis how quickly you could lose your comfort level in the game. In the fall, when hockey started up again after the summer break, it always felt at first as if he were using someone else's legs. Nothing seemed right.

Muck called them "hockey muscles." It didn't matter what shape you were in, those first few practices and games hurt, and you felt out of sorts. Muck said it was because your body had certain special muscles that only hockey itself could keep in shape. It would take nearly a month for Travis to get those muscles working the way they had the previous season.

When it felt right, Travis's skates felt like slippers, or socks. Or, even better, like skin-and-bone extensions of his own legs. He skated best, he knew, when he didn't think about skating at all. When he had to think about it, he felt stiff and awkward.

Same with shooting. When he had to think about the shot, it never went exactly as planned. When he just shot, it worked. He once read about Mike Bossy, who was likely the best pure "sniper" the NHL ever knew. He had nine straight fifty-goal-plus seasons before a bad back ended his career. Bossy said he never looked where he was shooting, he just shot. Somehow, wherever he was on the ice, his position in relation to the net was so deeply ingrained in his head that looking up to double-check was a waste of time.

Travis hadn't been on skates since the week before Christmas. Not much of a break, but enough to make his skates and his stick feel slightly *foreign* to him again. Not as bad as first thing in the fall, but enough that it worried him with such an important tournament about to begin. He was captain. He was expected to lead the team. He would have to be at the very peak of his abilities.

It felt good to skate around – "shake off the rust," Muck had said – and Travis began slowly. He glided about, doing wrist twists with his stick and stretching out each leg behind him, deliberately turning the late skate so that the blade dragged slightly along the ice surface.

Gradually, Travis found a little jump in his skating. He began digging harder in the corners, happy that he could hear his skates sizzle as he pushed out strong, certain that whoever was following him would see the long slashes his blades left in the fresh ice as he headed down rink.

The shooting came back just as surely. He began taking feeds from the corner and firing without much thought. He envied Dmitri, slipping in so effortlessly and using that wonderful deke to the backhand. Everyone, goalies included, always knew the deke was coming, but no one ever seemed able to do anything about it until the goalie's water bottle was flying through the air and Dmitri was doing a quick turn in the corner with his hands raised over his head.

He envied Sarah, too, already skating as if she were floating inches above the ice. Travis had heard

Muck tell his dad one day that Sarah had the best stride he had ever seen in a young person. Muck thought she had that same mysterious ability Paul Coffey and Scott Niedermayer used to show in the NHL, seeming somehow to pick up speed while simply gliding.

They ran a few drills, and then Muck blew his whistle sharp three times, calling the Owls to centre ice.

"Mr. Dillinger says we have something to settle," the coach told the players, most of whom were down on one knee in front of him.

"He suggests we have a crossbar competition to settle who gets the Gretzky seat."

The players all pounded their sticks on the ice in agreement. Travis joined in, even though he already had the treasured seat. In truth, he didn't care who sat on it, but he figured Nish shouldn't get it just because he'd thrown a hissy fit.

Mr. Dillinger laid out five pucks along the blue line while Muck chased the Owls into the two corners back of the goal. They would go one at a time, each player swooping out, curling hard as he or she picked up the first puck, coming in fast to shoot at the crossbar, then immediately cutting back to get the next puck, and the next, until all five shots had been taken.

It was more difficult than it sounded. To some

players coming in on an empty net, the crossbar looks as thin as dental floss. For others, the crossbar almost seems to be dancing, as if determined to avoid the shot. Some shoot too high, some too low. Some prefer backhand, some forehand. Some players seem to go weak in the arms when they know others are watching. And some, like Nish, like nothing better than to have an audience.

Travis loved crossbar shots. His one key superstition was to begin each game by nicking a shot off the bar in the warm-up. Hit the crossbar, and he'd have a good game; fail to hit it, and he could have a terrible game.

Travis also liked secretly to kiss the inside of his jersey, as close to the captain's "C" as he could, as he pulled the jersey over his head just before heading out onto the ice. He knew none of it made any sense, but what superstitions did?

Willie was the expert on hockey superstitions. Most people knew about growing playoff beards and about dollar coins – the Canadian "loonie" – buried at centre ice during important international matches, but Willie had a list of other superstitions that he sometimes rhymed off to the delight of the other Owls.

For example, every spring in Detroit, Red Wings fans throw an octopus onto the ice for good luck. An octopus, of course, has eight legs, and back in the days of the Original Six it used to take eight playoff wins to claim the Stanley Cup. Now it takes sixteen, but since scientists have yet to discover a sixteen-legged octopus hiding at the bottom of the ocean, the eight-legged version is still used.

Punch Imlach, who used to coach the Toronto Maple Leafs many years ago, used to wear a fedora hat while coaching — even though the games had been played indoors for decades. And one time, when a pigeon pooped on his hat while he was on his way to Maple Leaf Gardens, he left the white mess there for good luck. He didn't clean it off until his team lost a game.

Hall of Famer Phil Esposito wouldn't stay in a hotel room that had 13 in its number and would flip out if any of his teammates let their sticks cross in the dressing room. There were so many lucky rabbit feet and other charms hanging in Esposito's locker in the Boston Bruins' dressing room that he couldn't sit down to put on his equipment.

Wayne Gretzky would sprinkle baby powder on his new sticks before taping them, convinced that the stuff they put on babies' bums "softened" his passes during the game.

Patrick Roy used to talk to his goalposts and refused to "step" on any of the lines on the ice as he skated off between periods.

But one of the greatest superstitions of all time,

Willie said, was observed right here in this arena where the Owls were about to play. An Ottawa Senators player, Bruce Gardiner, became so upset one year about an unbreakable slump that he stormed into the washroom in full equipment and pretended to flush his cursed stick down the toilet. When Gardiner dramatically broke out of his slump that night by scoring, he tried the same thing next game and scored again. For the rest of the year, Gardiner flushed his stick down the toilet before each game, and many of his teammates joined in as they tried to end their own scoring droughts.

But Gardiner had nothing on Nish. Nish believed his good play was directly tied to never, ever, ever allowing his mother to wash his equipment. The more it stank, the better he believed he played. He even wore the same T-shirt under his equipment all year long – a once-white shirt that had stained yellow under the arms and was torn and bloodied and rotting right off him – but he loved it. To Nish, the T-shirt From Hell was as essential a piece of equipment as his skates and stick.

Muck began sending out the shooters, while Mr. Dillinger took care of setting up the pucks, a new row of five for each player.

Dmitri hit three in a row off the crossbar, all on the backhand, but then threw one high and one low. Three for five.

After Dmitri, it seemed no one could catch the backhand artist. Gordie hit two, both on big slappers. Sarah hit two on wrist shots. Sam hit one but missed two others by millimetres. Little Simon Milliken couldn't hoist the pucks high enough and slammed his stick hard on the ice in frustration.

There were eventually only two players left: Nish and Travis.

Muck was trying to decide which one to let go first. He knew what the seat meant to Nish, but he also knew whining and fighting was no way to get your way.

Muck nodded at Travis. "Lindsay," he said.

Travis looped out from the corner, acutely aware that all eyes were on him.

Ping! His first shot hit square off the crossbar and bounced away.

Ping! His second hit low and bounced straight down off the bar and into the net.

Two for two. He could hear sticks pounding on the ice in congratulations. His teammates were cheering for him. He didn't have to look to know Nish wasn't one of them.

Travis went to the backhand for his third shot and missed. He heard a few groans.

For his fourth, he tried a straight wrist shot and the puck skimmed off the bar and high into the glass.

Three out of four. The sticks slapped again on the ice.

Travis skated back and picked up the last puck. He could feel his legs shaking. This was his chance to take four and move ahead of Dmitri.

He tried the same shot. *Ping!* It bounced high off the crossbar and away.

Four out of five.

"*Go Trav!*" Sarah yelled from the corner. Others cheered as well.

"Nishikawa," Muck said, nodding in Nish's direction.

Nish slammed his stick on the ice as he started out. He chugged out to the blue line and cut hard, ice spraying as he turned back, and picked up the first puck.

He took two strides, went into his big exaggerated wind-up – "The Nishikawa," he called it – and boomed a puck straight off the crossbar. He looped back and repeated the shot exactly, right down to the loud *clang* off the bar.

Two for two.

"*Yo, Nish!*" Fahd called out. Sam scowled at him.

Nish had his third puck and was coming in, backhand. *Ping!*

Three for three. Several Owls pounded their sticks in recognition. Travis joined them. He was impressed.

For his fourth, Nish went back to his slapper, but he missed the shot slightly and the puck flipped in a slow arc and came in just under the bar.

Three for four.

He needed the last hit to tie Travis. He circled back, head down, and gathered up the fifth puck. He moved in, then stopped and stickhandled, looking down at the puck then up at the bar. It was more like a golfer preparing to make a chip onto the green than a hockey player about to take a shot.

"*No fair!*" Sam shouted. "*You have to be in motion!*"

Nish paid no attention. He looked up once more, then down, and heaved all his weight into a wrist shot.

The puck flew straight at the crossbar – and over.

The Owls erupted in cheers for Travis. He had won the Gretzky seat.

Nish slammed his stick angrily. "*It hit!*" he was screaming. "*It ticked off! I heard it!*"

Muck shook his head. "It missed."

"It just touched it!" Nish protested. "I *heard* it!"

Muck turned to the rest of the Owls. "Anyone else hear it, or is Mr. Nishikawa hearing things again?"

"Nothing!" Sarah shouted. "We heard nothing."

"*Liar!*" Nish screeched at Sarah as he skated away, slamming his stick on the ice and against the boards.

Muck blew his whistle. Once. Loudly. The Owls went completely silent. Even Nish.

"Off the ice, Nishikawa," Muck said, very quietly. "Go and get dressed."

"And stay out of Travis's locker!" Sam added.

Muck looked sharply at Sam, who reddened and instantly shut up. The coach blew his whistle again, twice.

"Shinny," Muck said. "Fifteen minutes."

The Owls cheered. Fifteen minutes of pure *play* hockey. It was what they all loved best, the time when they could try risky little tricks and not worry about Muck benching them for coughing up the puck.

Shinny was the only thing Nish liked about practice. It was when the big defenceman got to play puck hog and super hero and take slapshots from centre ice and try ridiculous, impossible things, like dropping the puck into his skates as he tried to go around the checker and then kicking it up to his stick once he was past.

Travis knew Nish had heard the cheers as he left the ice.

It had not been a good morning for Nish. He had lost twice. First the shootout, now fifteen minutes of shinny.

But then, Travis thought, I almost lost my life, thanks to Nish.

Nish flicked the television on as they were settling into their room at the motel, and they listened as a newsreader said Ottawa had become "an armed camp" with so many security forces brought in for the big trade summit. The news showed some film of presidents and premiers arriving on private jets and being escorted into the snow-covered capital by police escort. There were even police snipers placed on rooftops as the politicians arrived in the escorted convoys. The prime minister of Britain was already in town. So was the president of Russia. The president and vice-president of the United States were said to be on their way. The prime minister of Canada was headed out to the airport to await the landing of the U.S. president's jet, Air Force One, direct from Washington.

"Wow!" said Fahd. "This is *big*."

"This," corrected Nish, grabbing the remote off

the bedside table, "is *boring*. Where are the NHL highlights?"

The Owls were scheduled to play in one of the opening night matches in the big rink. The official schedule had them on right after the opening ceremonies: Screech Owls versus Portland Panthers.

The Owls would be playing their old rivals, and Travis would be up against two of his all-time favourite opposition players, Jeremy Billings and Stu Yantha.

If you had to pick an opening match to launch the Bell Capital Cup, you couldn't do better than that.

• • •

The Owls dressed in the visitors' dressing room, Travis somewhat sheepishly taking the Gretzky seat. He tried to tell himself it was only right. He had, after all, been first to sit on it. And then he had won the shootout, even if Mr. Dillinger had chosen the contest because he knew how Travis liked to practise hitting the crossbar. And Nish *had* acted the perfect jerk – so it was only right Nish didn't have it.

But still, Travis wished it was someone else. He hated being treated special. He hated the idea that people might think he considered himself better than he was. His notion of a perfect hockey game was to go play his heart out, assist on the winning goal, and then, the second his helmet and jersey came off, be unrecognizable as he headed back out to the tuck shop.

Nish, on the other hand, liked to go out, play whatever way he wanted, score all the goals, unassisted if possible, remove his helmet for the final glorious rush up the ice, and then, with the crowd cheering his victory, skate off the ice and head straight to the tuck shop, where fans would be lining up to buy purple slushies for their hero.

How on earth did they ever become friends? Travis wondered. And were they still friends after what had happened?

Mr. Dillinger was at the door, his faced flushed with excitement.

"We're on!" he told them. "Prepare yourselves for a shock!"

The Owls hurried after Mr. Dillinger, passing Muck in the hallway as the coach was finished filling out the game sheet and listing his starting lineup. Travis, having kissed his jersey and marvelled at the team's string of good fortune, hoped his line – Dmitri on right wing, Travis on left, Sarah at centre – would get the start. You never knew with Muck, and long ago Travis had learned there was no use guessing.

They turned left out of the hallway and came out

through the tunnel into such an explosion of light and sound and colour that Lars and Simon didn't see the red carpet laid out for the dignitaries and fell flat on their faces as they stepped onto the ice.

Scotiabank Place was packed. All the teams were there, nearly five hundred and fifty of them. With an average of almost twenty players per team, that was eleven thousand players alone. The screaming was amazing. The rink held more colours than a thousand rainbows: teams wearing their bright jerseys, parents and fans dressed up in team colours, too. The towering scoreboard was lit up with a video of the Owls making their entrance, Lars and Simon's great flop replayed and replayed, while rap music filled the arena with a beat so loud Travis felt it hammering in his own chest.

But that was only the beginning. After they had come out onto the ice and lined up, the light show began.

Travis had never imagined a peewee hockey tournament could open like this. The Bell Capital Cup was beginning with the same kind of show the Senators put on for the Stanley Cup finals. Spotlights were playing over the entire rink. Images of giant players were moving about the ice like movie stars projected on a screen, the huge players filling the ice surface and crawling up the boards and dancing through the cheering crowds.

"It's us!" Derek shouted.

Travis didn't catch on for a moment.

"It's me!" Nish shouted with delight. *"Me! Me! Me!"*

Travis finally saw what they were talking about. The video projected onto the ice was of Nish playing a game – it must have been from an earlier tournament. It was Nish for sure: the same telltale cock of the helmet, the wild, exaggerated slapshot, the big No. 44 on the back, just below the name, "NISHIKAWA."

"They choose their stars well, here," Nish hissed into Travis's ear. Travis could barely hear him over the crowd and the loud music, but he didn't need to. He knew that no matter how big the video enlarged Nish's head, it could never match the real thing.

There were other giant video-Owls skating over the ice. Travis caught sight of himself, and he marvelled at how gracefully the giant Sarah skated across the rink and high up into the crowd.

Then the video changed to the Panthers, causing a huge roar from another part of the crowd. Travis could recognize Billings without even seeing his number. The little defenceman, projected ten times his usual size, had such a distinctive skating style – almost as if he was sitting at a table about to start into his lunch instead of starting another rush up the ice.

And there was a giant Yantha with his heavy checks and hard, hard shot.

The music suddenly stopped and the arena went dark. The crowd hushed.

A single spotlight moved along the roof, picking through the rafters. Travis looked up, but he could make nothing out. The arena was completely silent, almost as if fifteen thousand people had decided to hold their breath at exactly the same time.

The spotlight was illuminating a small opening in the roof.

And then something fell. Fast.

Travis's heart leapt into his mouth. The object was big and orange and it was crashing to the ground. Had something gone wrong?

It was Spartacat, the Senators' colourful lion mascot. Spartacat was plummeting like a paratrooper who had forgotten to pack a chute. Someone screamed. The entire crowd gasped. Spartacat was crashing to the ice – to be killed in front of all these people.

But suddenly Spartacat slowed. He floated down to just above the rink and then dropped, perfectly, right at centre ice. Travis caught a glimpse of a thin wire being wound back up into the rafters. He'd been attached to an invisible line.

The crowd burst into cheers.

"Cool," Nish hissed in Travis's ear. "I'm gonna try that."

"You'd be chicken," Travis giggled. "You're terrified of heights, remember?"

Two very pretty young women in Senators' jerseys came out through the Zamboni chute. One carried a large bag, the other carried a shiny contraption that, on first glance, looked like a big gun.

It was the Master Blaster. The girl handed the gun to Spartacat while the other passed him a tightly wrapped T-shirt. With the T-shirt loaded into the gun, Spartacat turned and took aim at different points in the crowd as section after section roared in anticipation.

Whumph! The Master Blaster launched the T-shirt high into the air. As it arced into the crowd, men, women, and children along three rows of seats scrambled for the prize. It was as if Spartacat were firing thousand-dollar bills at them.

Whumph! Another T-shirt shot up into another section, causing the same mad scramble.

Whumph! Another.

Whumph! Whumph! Whumph!

"Awesome!" Nish yelled at Travis over the roar of the crowd. It looked like fun. Travis could see kids in the crowd looking at Spartacat as if he were as big a celebrity as Wayne Gretzky. He had never seen a wilder scene caused by one person — one, *cat*. Then again, he'd never seen anyone dive from the rafters of an arena and come up firing T-shirts into the crowd.

With all the T-shirts gone, the opening ceremony returned to more-usual formalities. Various dignitaries – the mayor of Ottawa, the organizers, the coach and general manager of the Senators – came out for the welcoming announcements and ceremonial faceoff, which Sarah would be taking against big Stu Yantha.

Spartacat was now handing out gifts to the two teams chosen to play the first game of the tournament, a Senators cap for each player, each one signed by a different member of the Ottawa Senators.

Normally, Nish would grab at such a prize to see if he'd got the best signature, and, if not, try and trick someone like Fahd into swapping. But he didn't seem the slightest bit interested. He was far more taken with Spartacat.

"I want to become a mascot!" Nish shouted up at the big furry lion.

Spartacat had already moved on to hand caps to Jenny and Jeremy, but when he had done with the goalies, he came back down the line, stopped behind Nish, and playfully knocked his helmet off, much to the delight of the crowd.

"Come see me after the game," a deep voice growled from somewhere inside the costume. "My dressing room's two over from the Zamboni chute."

Nish's scrambled to get his helmet back on and do up the chinstrap he'd foolishly left undone. "*Thanks,*" he shouted, though anyone who heard him thought he was thanking Spartacat for pointing out his helmet wasn't on right.

The opening ceremonies done with, the arena staff cleared the carpets from the ice, the lights came back on strong, and the referee prepared to drop the puck.

Sarah was lined up against Stu Yantha – only now, neither of them was smiling. Both were wound tight, determined to win the faceoff.

Travis looked over at Dmitri, ready for the fast break. He looked ahead and saw that Billings had already sensed Dmitri's plan and was ready to squeeze him out on any rush.

It was going to be quite a game.

It was going to be quite a tournament.

December 24

This is like taking candy from a baby. Too easy, too easy, too easy.

Personally, i'd rather they made it a challenge. i barely have to assign a single brain cell to dealing with these idiots.

i have the job. i got it easily. They never checked, of course. And now that i'm in, no one looks at me twice. i even have my own security card, so i can open any door in the place and go anywhere i please.

it's that simple. After 7/7, after it's over, and the world is reeling with shock, they will try

53

to make it sound next to
impossible. They'll have to. i
understand that. Their job is to
protect. But mine is to destroy.
And if i get my job done after
barely lifting a finger, what will
it say about how they did theirs?
So they'll lie and pretend that
whoever did this (please allow
me to introduce myself again:
it's Al) was some sort of sick
genius who must have spent
months, perhaps even years,
working out the plan.

Well, i don't mind the genius
part. And i could care less if
they think i'm sick — they're the
ones who are sick. But i do
want everyone to know how
stupefyingly simple this was to
pull off.

That's why the diary. i don't want
you to know who i am. But i do
want you to know how i did it.
The simplicity of it will make the
hurt all the greater.

You'll be looking for clues as you read this, i know. i'm half tempted to give it all away, it's so simple, but i think i'll string you along for a bit, just so the surprise is all the more stunning when you finally do wake up and see what happened, how easily it happened, and how brilliant it was for me to come up with my plan.

i am now inside the rink.

Where i need to be.

SARAH READ DMITRI'S PLAN PERFECTLY. SHE used her old faceoff trick of plucking the puck out of the air even before it landed, then turned so her body protected the puck from Yantha's attempted check and sent it sailing high down the ice.

Dmitri was already in full stride, timing it so he wouldn't cross the blue line before the puck and put himself offside. But Billings was ready. While Dmitri raced toward the Panthers' net, Billings charged straight up-ice toward the faceoff circle. When Sarah hoisted the puck, he leapt up, reaching high with his glove like a football linesman, and batted her pass out of the air.

The deflected puck bounced down between Lars and Fahd on defence. They turned quickly, but little Billings was already in full stride. He burst between the two Owls defenders, kicked the puck up onto his stick, faked a slapper that Jeremy stutter-skated out to get the angle on, and then simply walked around the helplessly falling Owls goalie and tucked the puck into the net as carefully as if he were putting a plate in the dishwasher.

It took the Owls to the end of the first period to get back in the game. Nish drove a hard shot from the point that bounced off a falling Billings's shinpad and looped high over the outstretched arm of the Panthers goalie for the Owls' first point.

In the second period, the Panthers went ahead again with a fantastic solo end-to-end rush by Yantha that ended with a high backhand into the near side.

Just before the buzzer, Travis found himself with the puck against the boards in his own end, and he chipped it past a pinching defenceman to give him and Dmitri a two-on-one, with Billings the Panthers' only player back.

Travis carried over centre and hit Dmitri early. Muck always said you give the puck to the man ahead of you, and you give it early, not when it's too late.

Dmitri took the pass at full speed, forcing Billings to shift his weight over to Dmitri's side, and Dmitri smartly used the opportunity to give the puck right back to Travis.

Travis had a clear route to the Panthers' net. He thought he'd take the shot, but then he held; the goalie had too good an angle on him. He held for what seemed too long, with Billings trying to get back to take out any return pass to Dmitri, and the

Panthers goalie staying with Travis for the shot.

Travis almost shut his eyes and prayed. If Sarah was true to course, she'd be coming up through the slot as fast as she could. He put the puck on his backhand and made a sweeping pass behind his own back – a play Muck hated – and hoped against hope.

Sarah was there. The pass was perfect. She one-timed it straight into the back of the Panthers' net, and the Scotiabank Place crowd roared its approval of the fancy goal. The Owls on the ice skated to the bench for the team high-fives and fist bumps.

Travis had to gather his nerve to look up at Muck. When he did, he saw Muck scowling back at him. And then smiling. Travis sighed. It had been a pretty goal – a beautiful goal – but it could just as easily have been an ugly turn in the game. If Sarah hadn't been there to take the pass, the Panthers would have broken out with the advantage. Travis had seen silly gambles fail enough times to know he couldn't risk that play again, especially against this team. And he also knew that Muck would allow him only the one chance.

In the third, with the game tied, Nish rose from his spot on the defence end of the bench and walked up to where Travis was sitting between Sarah and Dmitri.

"I'm going to try the big flipper," he said to Sarah and Dmitri. "One of you better be there."

Both nodded. Nothing more needed to be said. They were the team's two fastest skaters. If anyone could get to a loose puck, they could.

Nish found his chance late in the period. He picked up the puck and carried it behind his own net, rapping a pass to himself off the back of the net as a Panther tried to forecheck him. He then stepped out, faked a cross-ice pass to Willie, and instead turned and fired the puck into the air so high it looked like it was going to hit the score clock.

Dmitri was already on his way. With no centre-line offsides, Dmitri just had to make sure he didn't cross the Panthers' blue line before the puck.

Dmitri and the puck hit the blue line together. Nish's long pass bounced once as it hit the ice, and Dmitri caught it on the end of his stick. Billings was right behind him, having again seen what the play would be.

Dmitri shot across the blue line. Billings dived, swinging his stick at the puck in the hope of hitting it away. Dmitri brilliantly did a little flip with the puck so it was in the air as Billings's stick swung through, and he skipped over the stick as if he were jumping rope.

Dmitri was in, and clear. It was like watching an old movie, Travis thought, as he raced up-ice in case there might be a rebound.

Dmitri faked a shot, went to his backhand, and, in close, fired the puck so hard and high it seemed it could never get in.

But it did – the Panthers' water bottle spinning through the air and splashing against the glass as the red light came on.

Owls 3, Panthers 2. A win for the Owls.

"C'MON WITH ME."

Travis looked up, surprised. He had taken off his skates, gloves, jersey, and shoulder and elbow pads, and was sitting back in his locker – the Wayne Gretzky seat – with his eyes closed as he took in the moment.

At the beginning of a game, his nerves seemed to crackle and spark like his grandparents' fireplace up at the lake. He was so alive, so nervous, so worried, so excited, so wound up, it sometimes felt like all the pressure inside was going to blow out the top of his head like a whale spouting air.

But at the end of a game, he felt so incredibly different. Calm. His nerves dead. His chest heaving from the exertion, but feeling so relaxed and content he could almost fall asleep in full equipment. He knew, as usual, he had given his very best. Win or lose, he always tried to remember he had done his best. With that realization came a wonderful, happy satisfaction.

Travis loved both feelings. He liked to hang on as long as possible to that post-game sag that felt so good – just him in his locker, his equipment half-off, a cold bottle of orange Gatorade to finish before he packed up his bag for the bus ride home.

"*C'mon – hurry up!*"

It was Nish. Travis could not recall a time when Nish had been dressed before him, but there he was, sweaty black hair slicked back, perspiration still dripping off his chubby red face. He was ready to go, his bag packed.

"Where? What's up?" Travis asked.

"I'm to meet Spartacat, *remember*?" Nish hissed impatiently.

"You know where he is."

"You come too. You have to meet him."

Travis shrugged. He didn't really have to meet him – wasn't it better to know a mascot as a mascot, not the person inside the costume? – but he understood Nish's shyness. There was something just a little bit spooky about meeting a larger-than-life "character" in real life. He wouldn't want to go on his own either.

"Okay, give me a minute."

They found the door near the Zamboni entrance, in a long line of small dressing rooms marked "Officials" and "Staff" and "Coaches." On the door was a nameplate, "Spartacat," as if the mascot were a vice-president of the company or something equally important.

"You knock," Nish said.

Travis knocked, three quick raps

"A moment!" a muffled voice called from inside.

The two friends waited, fidgeting. They couldn't stay long. Mr. Dillinger had said the bus would be leaving for the hotel in twenty minutes.

The door opened, and a large, smiling man stood there. He had a shaved head and the bluest eyes Travis had ever seen. They seemed to stare right through you. Travis felt cold – a draft, surely, from the Zamboni chute.

"Mr. Spartacat?" Nish began.

"Not me," the smiling man laughed. "I'm Spartacat's assistant. His understudy. Whatever. I work with him."

"Come on in!" a deeper voice called from inside the dressing room.

The boys entered.

Spartacat had lost his head. It lay on a table, still smiling its cartoon smile. Spartacat's body had grown a new head, a human head, with thick, curly dark hair and laughing eyes. The man who played Spartacat was still in the body part of the mascot suit. He was covered in sweat, and he, too, was gulping down a Gatorade.

"You wouldn't believe how hot it gets in here," the man said. "I'm Rudy, by the way. And this is Mr. Smith – John – Spartacat's new associate."

"I'm in training," John Smith said, with a big, open smile.

"I'm Wayne Nishikawa," Nish said, "but everyone just calls me Nish."

"I'm Travis," said Travis.

"You boys keen on becoming mascots?" Rudy asked.

"I am," Nish jumped in. "Travis is my best friend."

Travis said nothing. He had to bite off a smile. What if he told Spartacat that his best friend had tried to choke him to death earlier in the day?

"It's tough work," John said. "That's why the team has hired me to help Rudy. We're actually going to have *two* Spartacats for this tournament. But please don't tell anyone. Promise?"

They both promised.

"The tournament has just gotten way too big for one mascot to handle," said Rudy. "We've got games going on at more than a dozen rinks in Ottawa. It's a full-time job just working the Sensplex. Seen it yet?"

The boys shook their heads. But they had heard about the Bell Sensplex. Four ice surfaces in one building. One of the rinks Olympic size. The complex even had a full-size indoor soccer field and a video-game room the size of a schoolroom. Data, the Owls' top video-game player, could hardly wait to get there.

"You're going to love it," Rudy said. "Like to see Spartacat's stuff?"

"You bet!"

Rudy showed them the costume closet. "I have three full Spartacat outfits," he explained. "Have to, in case one gets a tear in it, or if one of our more enthusiastic fans dumps beer over my head. It's happened."

He showed the boys a scrapbook of Spartacat at charity events, Spartacat visiting the children's hospital, Spartacat with the rest of the NHL mascots – including Carlton the Bear from the Toronto Maple Leafs, Sabretooth from Buffalo, Vancouver's Fin the Whale, Montreal's Youppi, Tampa Bay's Thunderbug, and the league's very first team mascot, Calgary's Harvey the Hound – at the annual All-Star Game. There were also photographs of Spartacat with a number of hockey celebrities, including Wayne Gretzky, Sidney Crosby, and Paul Kariya.

"Paul Kariya's my cousin," Nish boasted.

"Is that right?" said Rudy.

No, it wasn't right, but Travis let it go. At the Quebec City peewee tournament, Nish had concocted this whole idea that he was Paul Kariya's cousin, and now he'd said it so often he seemed to believe it himself. Travis thought it had to do with jealousy, Travis's father being a distant cousin of

"Terrible" Ted Lindsay, who had led Detroit to all those Stanley Cups and was in the Hockey Hall of Fame. That, or else the fact that both Nish and Paul Kariya were part-Japanese, which made them related, sort of . . . in Nish's squirrelly mind, anyway.

"Can we see the Master Blaster?" Nish asked.

"Sure," Rudy said. He opened up a foot locker beside the costume closet. Inside were all sorts of strange things, including something that looked, to Travis, like a giant slingshot.

"Is that what I think it is?" he asked.

"A slingshot?" said Rudy. "Yep." He pulled it out of the box. He handed John, his assistant, one end, and he took the other. They stretched it halfway across the room.

"I get the girls to do this part," Rudy explained. "Then I place a T-shirt or whatever in the sling and – so long as they're able to hold it – I can fire it from the ice surface all the way into the upper bowl."

"I'd love to have something like that for Mr. Twindle's science class," Nish said.

Travis saw Rudy smile and nod. Poor Rudy, Travis thought. He's probably thinking Nish would like to demonstrate for the class some principle of physics. Nish, of course, would be thinking nothing of the sort. He'd be imagining having his partners-in-crime, Fahd and Wilson, on both sides, stretching out the rubber bands, while he packed a mittful of soaking-wet toilet paper into the sling so he could fire it over poor fumbling Mr. Twindle's head and onto the blackboard.

Rudy put the slingshot away and pulled out the gleaming Master Blaster. This was what Nish had been waiting for. His eyes grew larger and took on a familiar glint. It was the look of Nish scheming – and Travis didn't like it.

The Blaster was about as long as Rudy's arm and had the shine of polished chrome. It had a large open tube at one end where "missiles" such as hot dogs could be inserted. At the other end, there was a lever to cock the gun for firing and a large trigger to fire off the missile once Spartacat had picked the spot in the stands where he wanted the prize to go. It looked a bit like an old wartime bazooka, a bit like a paint-ball gun.

"This is what I'm using more and more these days," Rudy said. "Better range and faster than the slingshot. I can fire shirts or hot dogs from one end of the rink to the other with amazing accuracy. The most fun is to fire them into the luxury boxes. You haven't seen anything till you've watched business-men in suits who are sitting in three-hundred-dollar seats fight each other to the death for a three-dollar hot dog."

"How's it work?" Nish asked.

"Compressed air," Rudy explained. I use these little CO_2 cartridges and they provide the power. The rest is just loading up, cocking, and firing. Very much like a gun, really – only you can't do any damage with a T-shirt!"

He handed the Master Blaster to John, who was giggling at Rudy's little joke, and John carefully put it away.

"I want to drop from the ceiling," Nish said.

"It's called rappelling," Rudy explained. "It was developed by mountaineers for scaling down cliffs. The military picked it up for assaults on occupied buildings. It's simple enough, so long as you have the right equipment."

"Can you teach me?" Nish asked.

"I could," Rudy said, "but it's not for kids to play with – it's for the act."

"What if I had a costume? You know – a miniature Spartacat."

Rudy laughed. "Sparta-*kitten?*"

"Yeah, sort of . . ."

"That would be something," Rudy said, shaking his head. "I suppose it might be possible to trim down one of the extra costumes."

"Not a good idea," interrupted John. "They'd never allow it. Too risky. The insurance people would have a fit."

"Ah, c'mon, relax," said Rudy. "What they don't know won't hurt them. He can at least hang around a bit and see what we do."

"*I can?*" Nish shouted. "You'd let me?"

"Sure, why not? Just watch, though, and don't do anything without my permission. I'll see how we might alter a costume to fit you. Might be just the thing to spark up this kids' tournament."

Travis noticed that John wasn't as keen on the idea as Rudy. In fact, John seemed very much against it, and Travis could sympathize with him on that point. Rudy had no idea how crazy or out of control Nish could get. And the chances of Nish doing something very stupid without permission were, well, very high.

With a grim look, John turned to put things away. He seemed somewhat put off by this intrusion. John, after all, was the new assistant. He was the one in training. He was the backup. And now, in the midst of having to learn everything about being a mascot, he had to deal with Nish, too.

December 27

i am iN, i am iN, i am iN. iN. where i
Need to me. iN. where i shouldN't
be. iN. where i caN. do the most
damage wheN. the day comes.

it was too easy, i said, aNd i was
right. i Needed a test, aNd today i
think i fouNd it. EverythiNg has
beeN. goiNg so smoothly, so
perfectly, so absolutely right.
i get Nervous wheN. thiNgs go
so well, so i actually welcome
the odd speed bump oN. the way
to where i have to get.

This oNe i shall squash like a
traNsport trailer hittiNg aN. empty
pop caN. oN. the road. NothiNg
will keep me from 7/7, the Day of

Reckoning. Nothing. What will come about that day, on the first day of the first month of the New Year, will stand with the planes hitting the Twin Towers on 9/11 and the London subway bombers of 7/7.

9/11.

7/7.

1/1.

And this one will be even more devastating. Not only will it take those so-called "innocent lives" (innocent, my eye – all are equally guilty), but it will take other lives, public lives, and in such a dramatic fashion that 1/1 will one day stand above 9/11 and 7/7. it will be forever marked as the Day the World Changed.

For the better. For necessary reasons.

They will eventually be forgotten.
i will never be forgotten. — even
if, with luck, i get out and am
never ever found.

That is the reason for this
diary. if i have vanished, this
diary will be my witness. And
then people will know how easy
it was. And how easy the next
one can be. And how they can
never, ever again dare to sleep
with both eyes closed.

i will have changed the face of
humanity.

Me. Al.

So long as i squash this little
road bump.

9

"PERFECT!"

Travis was roused from sleep by Nish's high-pitched voice.

"That's absolutely *perfect!*"

He rolled over and blinked hard, several times. He'd been fighting a head cold and his eyes were gumming up a bit. He'd have to wash them with warm water to see properly.

But he could still see well enough to know Nish was sitting on his bed, Data was pulled up beside him with his laptop open, and Willie was directing them to a website.

"This is the same place I found out about the world's longest fart," Willie was explaining. "It's not Guinness – so it's not official – but I have a hunch this entry here might be true."

Data read it out. "Largest Mass Mooning in History. It is estimated that two thousand protesters in Sweden gave United States President George W. Bush the greatest mass mooning of all time."

"*Two thousand!*" Nish squealed. "*That's nothing!*"

"What's going on?" Travis said in a sleepy voice.

"Nothing that concerns you," Nish said. "Go back to sleep."

But Travis couldn't. When those two words — "Nish" and "mooning" — came together, they invariably spelled trouble. Nish's lifetime ambition, he always said, was to moon more people than anyone in history. He'd almost pulled it off, too, in New York City one New Year's Eve. Nish had streaked in Vancouver and in Sweden. He had mooned from the team bus — out of sight, surprisingly, of Mr. Dillinger's rear-view mirror — and he had mooned his teammates so often in the dressing room no one paid the slightest attention anymore whenever he walked in, dumped his equipment bag, turned his back, and dropped his pants to offer what he liked to call "The Official Nish Greeting."

"What *exactly* are you planning, now?" Travis asked in what he thought of as his "captain's voice." But he sounded too much like a parent, or a teacher, and he knew it.

"Well, if it isn't Old Woman Lindsay, just up from her nap," Nish said. "Go back to sleep. The real world's too exciting for you."

"No," Travis argued, unwinding himself out of his sheets. "What's up?"

"You heard the man," Nish said. "How many was it, Data?"

"Two thousand," Data answered. "That's the biggest mass mooning in history."

"What's the biggest number *mooned*, though?" Nish asked.

Data flicked down through the website. "No numbers. Don't know."

"Well," Nish announced grandly. "I can promise you, twenty thousand people at a live event would be a world record."

"Where are you going to find twenty thousand people to look at your ugly butt?" Travis asked, shaking his head.

"The final," Nish said. "They're expecting the same number that turns out for an NHL game."

"You'd never get out of your hockey pants," Travis giggled.

Nish dismissed him with a shake of his head. "Fool," he said. "I'd float down from the skies like one of those cute little angels you see in old paintings."

Travis didn't need an explanation. Nish was thinking about Spartacat's grand entrance.

"You can't possibly be serious," Travis said.

"Dead serious," Nish countered.

"Dead is right," added Willie. "You slip, and just think what you might land on!"

"I'm being tutored by the world's Number One mascot," Nish said snippily. "It can't miss."

"You're an idiot," Travis said.

"Go back to sleep, old woman," Nish snapped, turning his attention back to the computer screen.

TRAVIS WAS EATING HIS BREAKFAST — FRUIT
Loops swamped in milk, toast with peanut butter,
and a large orange juice – when the wheels of Data's
chair bumped up against his table.

Data had a copy of the *Ottawa Citizen* on his lap.
He was tapping a long finger on a front-page story.

WORLD LEADERS TO PUT
DIFFERENCES ON ICE FOR NEW YEAR'S

The 22 world leaders attending Ottawa's economic summit are going to a hockey game.

Prime Minister Denise LeBlanc announced
Thursday that the gathering of world leaders
currently under way in Ottawa will break New
Year's Day to attend the final match of the Bell
Capital Cup at Scotiabank Place.

The purpose is threefold, LeBlanc told
reporters at the Ottawa Conference Centre.

"It is, first and foremost, to show our visitors the game Canada has given to the world," she said. "But also to underline the importance of a healthy population to a healthy economy.

"These young men and women playing in this year's Bell Capital Cup will one day be leaders in their own countries. We want them to know that there are grown-ups dedicated to making the world they will inherit a healthier and wealthier place."

"Wow!" Travis said, handing back the newspaper to Data. "The prime minister is coming to the game?"

"And the president of the United States," said Data. "And the heads of Russia, France, Britain, Australia, Germany, Finland, Sweden, Norway. Twenty-two of them in total. The press coverage will be incredible."

"It would sure be something to make that final," Travis said, returning to his Fruit Loops.

"I've got a feeling we will," said Data. "I just wish I could play in it."

Travis said nothing. What could he say? Everyone wished so much that Data could go back to playing the way he once had, the slow and steady defence-man everyone could count on. But all they could do was hope for some medical breakthrough, some miracle that would one day allow Data to walk and skate again. At least Muck and Mr. Dillinger made sure he was still on the team. He might not be able to skate, but Data had become a valuable assistant coach – as important as any player on the team.

● ● ●

The Owls played that morning at the Sensplex. They were on one of the smaller ice surfaces, but it was still perfect. The ice was hard and fast, with no chips to cause pucks to bounce away and no sticky parts to infuriate the defencemen at the start of each period.

There was room in the stands for only a couple of hundred people, but that was more than enough space, as hardly any of the Owls' parents had made the trek to Ottawa, and the other team, the Brighton Bulldogs, had come all the way from England, so not many of their parents had been able to afford the trip.

Travis knew from the warm-up that it would be an Owls victory. And not just because he rang a shot off the crossbar on his very first try. Sometimes he could tell just by watching the other team before the game.

For one thing, the Brighton team had no set warm-up patterns, which meant they weren't well coached. Instead, their coach was yelling out instructions from the bench, which was something Muck would never do. The Owls knew their own warm-up routine by heart, and they did it all – passing, two-on-ones, shots from all angles, jamming the net, hard skating at centre – without one of them having to be told the order of events. It was as familiar to them as brushing their teeth.

Or, in Nish's case, as familiar as passing gas at embarrassing moments – as Nish considered brushing his teeth as important as cleaning his hockey equipment.

But there was more to it than just their lack of organization during the warm-up. Travis noticed some of the British players were stiff legged and couldn't corner equally well in both directions. That was a sign of too much public skating, when everyone had to go in the same counter-clockwise direction. And their shots were not quick snaps but big windup slapshots which told the goaltender exactly where the shooter was hoping to go. That allowed goalies like Jeremy or Jenny to gamble, coming out farther than normal to cut down angles.

Muck didn't start Travis's line. He went, instead, with Derek and Gordie and put Jesse on the right wing. They scored on the first shift, big Gordie Griffith firing a puck from the corner that Derek very neatly deflected off his stick blade high into the Brighton net.

Muck didn't put Sarah and Travis and Dmitri out second, either, but went with a third line of Simon, Andy, and Willie.

They also scored, Willie going in on a quick break and, instead of shooting, dropping the puck back to Simon, who slipped around the goaltender and dropped the puck into the net.

Travis's line didn't even go third. Instead, Muck decided to go back to Derek's line. They nearly scored, with Gordie Griffith getting the puck back to Sam on the point, and Sam hammering a hard shot off the crossbar.

Travis could sense Muck was standing behind him. He and Sarah turned at the same time. Muck was leaning down.

"I want you guys just to practise your passing and forechecking," their coach said. "I don't need goals from you today."

The three first-liners – Travis, Sarah, and Dmitri – all nodded. They understood. Unlike so many other coaches, Muck would never run up the score on a weak team. He was against it even if goals-for and goals-against might determine which teams met in the final. In Muck's opinion, if the Owls couldn't get to the final, fair and square, without doing anything stupid like embarrassing another team on purpose, then they didn't want to be there.

Travis liked that about Muck. And besides, the three enjoyed practising their passes almost as much as making every pass, every shot, count.

It was a good workout. They held the puck and tried some patterns that Travis could tell hypnotized even the Brighton coach. At one point, just before a faceoff, he noticed the coach writing something down on an index card. Perhaps it was a play he had just learned from the three first-liners. Travis hoped so.

The final score was 5-0. It could have been 15-0, or maybe even 25-0, but 5-0 was fine by Muck. Sometimes, in large tournaments, a team got placed in the wrong division. It had happened to the Bulldogs, who should have been placed much lower. Perhaps the Brighton team had thought they were better than they actually were and recommended the level themselves. Who knew?

Muck wasn't much interested in talking about the game. He was far more interested in the game coming up on the big Olympic ice surface at the Sensplex — a game the Owls wouldn't even be playing.

"I want us to sit together and watch this next match," Muck said.

Travis heard a small groan come out of Nish, who had been eyeing the big video room upstairs.

"Kazakhstan is playing a team from the U.S.,"

Muck said. "I want you kids to know there's more than one way to play this game."

They sat along the top couple of rows of the biggest rink in the Sensplex. They were all wearing their Screech Owls jackets and looked like a team, but Travis knew the Owls still appeared like amateurs compared to some of the teams from places like Toronto and Detroit. Some of those teams had brand-new team jackets and caps and even team track suits with their names and numbers stitched on. Travis had heard that a couple of the teams had buses nicer than the ones famous entertainers toured in. And rumour had it that some teams charged parents more per year for their kids to play than it cost to send a child to university.

"Country club teams," Muck called them, and never bothered to hide his disdain. He believed hockey was a team sport, meaning each player was equal to the next, regardless of ability or family income. As soon as you made it a sport for the wealthy, he said, you eliminated the players who came from working-class roots. He would then rhyme off the names of NHL stars who might never have played the game if it had been up to some of these modern peewee teams: Gordie Howe, Bobby Orr, Mario Lemieux, Wayne Gretzky . . .

One thing was certain, the Kazakhstan Komets were not a country club team. Some of the Owls had seen them arrive, wearing ill-fitting "suits" that were in some cases just a coat and pants that didn't match. To Travis, they looked like they were going to a funeral rather than a hockey game. They had no flashy team jackets with their crest on the front and their numbers and names on the arms. Their equipment was basic and out of date. They had no composite sticks, for one thing. The Komets' sticks were all wooden. And the skates, Travis thought, looked like his father's old pair. Like something out of the Dark Ages.

The Owls were laughing to themselves as they watched the Kaz kids with their old equipment move onto the ice. But they stopped laughing not long into the warm-up. It was as if every kid on the Kazakhstan team skated like Dmitri and Sarah. Travis had never seen an entire team with such fluid, graceful skating abilities. And no slapshots during warm-up. None. All quick wristers.

"They don't take slapshots!" Fahd laughed. "What *wusses!*"

"They don't take slapshots in warm-ups because they don't want to break their sticks," Muck corrected. "You'd be the same if your stick cost your parents a week's wages. But if they have a chance in a game, they'll take one. Just you wait and see."

It was a game unlike anything Travis had ever seen. It wasn't as if the American opposition, the Buffalo Bears, weren't good. They were very good – fast and tough and well coached. But the Bears didn't have a chance.

Travis wasn't quite sure what he was seeing, but it didn't look like hockey as he knew it. In a way, it looked familiar, but he couldn't quite place it. The Kaz team would attack, then roll back, then come again, and again, and again in waves, each time turning back at the Buffalo blue line until they saw the opening they needed. If a hole appeared in the Buffalo line, they would break through and go in on net, always with the slight advantage. Two-on-one. Three-on-two. Four-on-three.

And then the passing would begin. Always in one motion. Always with a clear sense of where the other player was. Passes that seemed blind but went exactly where they needed to go.

The first three goals were all the same. The Americans got so bamboozled by the intricate passing plays that the scorer was in alone, once even behind the goaltender with the net lying empty.

When the Americans regrouped, turning to a one-on-one defence rather than a zone defence, the Kaz kids also regrouped. Instead of passing until they were in and clear, they kept dropping the puck as they moved forward, each puck-dropper then discreetly taking out his checker with a little hip brush or by strategic placement of his body to keep the American from going for the puck.

They worked this travelling cycle until, finally, one of the Kaz defencemen had a clear shot to the net. He wound up and slapped it.

Goal! Straight over the shoulder of the stunned Buffalo goaltender.

"Holy cripes!" shouted Sam. "That guy's got a cannon!"

"Check the shots against the score," Muck told them.

Travis looked up. Score: 4–0. Shots: 4 for Kazakhstan, 12 for Buffalo.

"Four goals on four shots?" Fahd said "Impossible!"

"Not impossible at all when you play like that," Muck said. "You recognize it, don't you? You've seen it played before."

The Owls shouted out names of hockey teams, but Muck just shook his head. "It's not even hockey," Muck said. "It's soccer – or, as they prefer to call it, *football.*"

Travis now knew why he thought he'd seen this game played before. His grandfather often watched English soccer on television and was fanatical about watching the World Cup every four years. He was always going on about brilliant plays and attacks that neither Travis nor his father could appreciate. But the patterns had been the same. The same circling and waiting for an opening; the same dropping back, again and again, until one player had the opening for that critical shot.

"This is how the Russians played in the 1972 Summit Series," Muck told them. "And the greatest hockey game every played was New Year's Eve, 1975," he continued. "The Red Army versus the Montreal Canadiens. Everybody remembers it was a 3–3 tie, but the far more interesting statistic was the shots. The Canadiens outshot the Russians 49 to 13. Think about that: 49 shots for three goals, 13 shots for three goals. A tie game.

"The Russians don't play like that anymore. But these kids do. They're coached by old Russian players from the 1970s, and they play the old style. It's a different game, and you're lucky to get a chance to see it."

Travis was fascinated. He had never seen such puck control. Never seen such intricate teamwork. Each player was like a carbon copy of the next. Each had the same skills as the next. Any player could score the goal, it seemed. There were no individual stars; they were *all* stars.

He hoped that before the Bell Capital Cup was over, he would have a chance to see Kaz hockey down on the ice.

Back at the hotel that evening, the Owls were in the midst of what seemed like the world's biggest mini-stick hockey tournament. They had set up a "rink" that took up the entire second-floor hall. Data was in goal at one end, guarding the open door to the room he was sharing with Jesse, Gordie, and Wilson; and Sam was in goal at the other end, guarding the door to the room she was sharing with Sarah and Jenny.

Travis's team was ahead approximately 42-39 when Mr. Dillinger came through the doors from the stairway and clapped his hands together, hard. He was puffing from the climb and seemed to be jiggling with delight.

"First thing tomorrow morning, we're skating the canal!" he announced. "Bed early, up early, on the ice early. And don't forget your long underwear!"

The Owls cheered his announcement and decided to end the mini-stick game with the usual "Next goal wins!" It came almost instantly, as Jenny, playing out, cuffed the little ball off the wall on a perfect angle. The "puck" bounced between Data's wheels and into his room.

Game over.

Travis wanted to get to sleep fast so morning would come quicker. His roommates, however, weren't being co-operative. Nish had the sports highlights on, staring blankly at the screen as NHL goals were scored, impossible basketball shots went in, and skiers flew down mountains. Lars and Fahd were talking excitedly about the canal skate.

"It's going to be freezing," Lars said. "I'm wearing my two pairs of long johns."

"The big thing is supposed to be the wind," said Fahd. "If you're going with it, it's an easy skate. If it's against you, it's like trying to skate uphill."

Nish had begun to do his usual last-minute flick through all the channels. He passed, then returned to, a channel showing people on a beach using para-sails instead of powerboats to wakeboard over the surf. They would let the sail rise high like a kite into the wind and then it would whisk them up onto the surface of the water and away. Some of them skimmed so quickly over the water that occasionally they rose above the crests of the waves and were actually airborne.

"Neat," Nish announced. "Look at this!" Lars and Fahd turned their attention to the television.

Travis turned his attention to dreaming of the canal. He flicked off his light, ducked in under the covers, and was instantly asleep.

THE OWLS BOARDED MR. DILLINGER'S OLD BUS – "*It's freezing!*" screamed the ones heading for the back, where the heater had no effect – and headed for Dow's Lake, where they would put their skates on and enter the canal. It was early in the morning, but already thousands of skaters were out to enjoy the deep freeze, which usually came sometime after the holiday was over.

Mr. Dillinger was in charge. Muck had decided to go instead to the National War Museum. When they dropped him off in front of the museum, their old coach had seemed as wide-eyed and excited as a kid with a ticket for the Stanley Cup final.

When they arrived at Dow's Lake, Travis looked out at the skaters through a hole he had wiped clear in the frost-covered window of the bus. The frost blurred his view a little, but that only made it more beautiful. The snow and ice were dazzling in the sunshine. The colours of the early-morning skaters were so vibrant, the frosted-over scene looked like a modern-art painting, with dabs of different paint still running on the canvas.

It was cold enough, when they got off the bus, to lock Travis's nostrils when he tried to breathe through his nose. He had to alternate between nose and mouth, but the air felt so fresh and alive that he didn't mind.

They laced up in a big tent and stepped gingerly out onto the ice. All the Owls felt slightly awkward, almost as if skating in winter clothes without a stick required different skills than skating in full hockey equipment with a stick in your hands. It took a few minutes to adjust, but soon they were darting all over the ice where it spread from the canal into the much-wider Dow's Lake.

Travis was surprised at how smooth the ice surface was. He had often skated on outdoor rinks, and he knew how quickly real ice could cut up, how easily scabby flaws could form, and how common it was for large cracks to appear. But this ice seemed flawless.

Every so often, he skated by something that looked like an ice-fishing hole with orange paint around the opening to warn skaters. The openings, however, had already frozen over hard. Of course, Travis realized. The holes were opened at night by the maintenance crews to pump water from below and flood the surface of the canal. It was not only the world's longest skating rink, it was, at this moment, the world's *smoothest* skating rink. But how different this skating rink was. When Travis went public skating in Tamarack, music would be blaring over the public address system, and the skaters all had to go in the same direction to avoid collisions.

Not here. There was no music, yet the air was full of sound: the noise of kids screaming and laughing, of parents calling for their children, of dogs barking, of bells jingling on the reins of the horse-drawn sleighs offering rides along the frozen canal.

And it was up to each skater to decide which way to go. Mainly, however, those skating toward Dow's Lake kept more or less to the left, and those, like the Owls, heading from the lake down towards the Chateau Laurier in the centre of the city, some seven kilometres away, kept more or less to the right.

Travis and Sarah headed out into open, new ice, their blades flicking up ice particles as they dug in, their hard strides marked behind them as surely as, in summer, a wake followed the boats cutting through the water in precisely this same place on the canal.

The Owls darted and flew about the canal, for a while playing keep-away with Fahd's thick Toronto Maple Leafs toque, only handing it back when he said he couldn't feel his ears.

They skated down past the football stadium and

under bridges, and soon they came within sight of the castle-like Chateau. Travis marvelled at all the different skaters: youngsters just learning; young parents pushing sleds holding thick, colourful bundles containing babies; older people moving with a slow grace that made Travis wish his grandparents could be there.

Nish caught up to a speed skater, an elderly man with old, long-bladed skates and a relaxed, almost swinging skating style – knees bent, back curled, head straight up, hands clasped behind the back. Nish began following directly behind, imitating the old man's delightful motion.

Nish looked ridiculous. His gut seemed even larger than usual – how many fleeces had he put on under his ski jacket? Travis wondered – and as Nish began skating like the old man, his belly stuck out in a way that made him look like a duck.

Several other Owls joined in, until the speed skater was the engine of a long, twisting train, the Owls forming little railway cars all the way back to Derek, the caboose. The old man looked back, a big smile on his face. Then he dug in, and in an instant he was gone, his stride pushing him away so fast, none of the Owls in their short-bladed hockey skates could keep up.

"I'm gonna get a pair of those skates for hockey," Nish vowed.

"They're illegal for hockey," Travis warned him.

Nish looked at Travis as if his friend had taken leave of his senses. "So's hooking and holding, goof – but how do you think I play the game?"

Travis shook his head and took off on his own, hooking up with Sam, Dmitri, and Sarah for some quick skating along the sides, where there were fewer skaters. They turned a corner and hit the wind like a wall. They had to dig in hard just to keep going. This was no "play day," Travis realized; Muck and Mr. Dillinger were no fools. This was better than any practice. More fun, too.

They skated as far as the National Arts Centre and stopped at one of the kiosks serving cinnamon "beaver tails" and hot chocolate before heading back. Travis thought the beaver tails looked like pizza crusts without the meat and sauce, but they were sweet as doughnuts.

"It'll be a lot easier going back," said Sam. "The wind will be with us."

"The wind's picking up," noted Sarah. "I'm sure glad we're not trying to skate this direction now."

They set out as a foursome. Travis, Sam, Sarah, and Dmitri all held hands and fanned out across the ice, letting the wind catch them and carry them along. They could move at a fair clip without even trying.

"*Neat!*" shouted Sam.

"*Would you look at that!*" Sarah shouted, looking back.

The four skaters stopped and turned. Nish had unzipped his jacket, and Fahd and Lars were pulling out something large and white he'd been keeping inside it. It hadn't been extra fleeces making Nish look fatter than usual. It was this thing, whatever it was.

Nish and the others carefully unfolded the object they had pulled from his ski jacket. It was a big bed-sheet from the hotel.

The boys had attached lines to the four corners, which connected to a long coil of rope.

Lars and Fahd were holding the sheet out, the corners whipping as the wind tried to catch it. Nish unwound the coil of rope, then tied it around his waist.

"He's *not!*" Dmitri said.

"He *is!*" shouted Sam with a squeal.

"He's *crazy!*" added Travis.

Nish gave the thumbs-up, and Fahd and Lars let the wind fill the sheet. It swelled at once with the hard breeze flowing up the canal, and Nish suddenly shot out from the crowd that had gathered around.

"KA-WA-BUNG-GA!!!" Nish screamed.

He shot by the four Owls with a huge smile on his beet-red face. Travis had rarely seen him look so triumphant – and Travis had seen many, many such looks on his best friend's face.

Nish ripped by . . . and he began to *soar!*

The wind had gusted from somewhere beyond the Chateau Laurier, dipped down into the trough of the canal, and punched hard like a fist into the open sheet, lifting Nish off the ice and into the air.

He was airborne!

He was also helpless. He had tied the rope tight around his waist and now was frantically trying to loosen it and escape. But it was too late. The wind gusted harder, and Nish, having harnessed its power, had to go along for the ride – for however long it lasted.

People were screaming. Some were pointing their cellphones in Nish's direction, hoping to capture a photo of the flying skater.

Nish rose higher in an updraft. Travis could hear him screaming, his high-pitched shriek a familiar note in a full orchestra of screaming and shouting from along the ice. The world's largest skating rink had come to a complete halt. People stood still and stared up in awe.

Nish flew even higher, now four storeys or more above the crowd. As he flew along the canal, the skaters in his path parted, fearing he would release himself and drop like a sack of cement wearing two sharp skate blades.

Nish screamed and the wind changed direction, buckling the sheet in half. The sheet fluttered and folded, and Nish plummeted to earth.

He came down hard on the roof of the nearest kiosk, smashing through the structure and landing smack on a table stacked with dough for the day's production of beaver tails.

The thick, soft dough, police would later tell the *Ottawa Citizen*, probably prevented more serious injury to the boy.

Still, Nish ended up with a twisted knee and a nose full of dough. His nose would be unplugged by a nurse with a warm washcloth, but the knee would take longer. The doctor at the children's hospital advised him to stay off it for two to three days.

No hockey.

The Screech Owls had just lost their Number One defenceman.

December 28

i have a small problem.

Small — that's another clue for you.

Not to worry. i shall deal with it. Everything is falling into place. i have found, as i recorded already, exactly the "job" i need to execute this amazingly simple, stunningly brilliant plan.

When all is done, people will cringe in anticipation of what might come next. Perhaps nothing will come next. Nothing will need to. The beauty of an act like this is the terror it sets in motion. There is really no need to do anything more. That, you see, is the true beauty of terrorism. Not what happened, but what might happen next. i can spend the rest of my life on a beach in Hawaii, not lifting a finger, and still cause the world to live in fear, every single day.

Brilliant? You bet it is. Just you wait and see.

First, though, my "small" problem. i have never liked children. i was never one myself — merely a miniature version of the person i am today. Then again, i was never human, either, so i am afraid i do not relate to human children at all.

This one is particularly annoying.

i need him out of the way.

NISH HAD NEVER KNOWN SUCH GLORY. HE WAS propped up in his bed, a bag of ice wrapped around his knee, a couple of bandages on his nose and lip, surrounded by copies of newspapers with front-page stories on what the *Ottawa Citizen* was calling "The Flying Hockey Player."

The *Ottawa Sun* even had a photograph of Nish's bulky body smashing through the roof of the beaver-tail kiosk. "Two Minutes for Boarding!" the headline screamed.

But it was going to be much more than two minutes. Muck was furious. No one could understand how Nish could be so stupid as to tie the rope around his waist. But Travis figured it was quite obvious really: Nish wanted to be able to wave to the people cheering him as he sailed down the ice.

He wasn't allowed to play at least until the final – if the Owls somehow happened to make it that far without him. But he was free to move about, so long as he iced the knee regularly and stayed off skates.

For Nish, this was a glorious opportunity to spend more time with his new friend Spartacat and learn the tricks of the mascot trade.

"We reach the final," he told Travis, "I'll have to decide whether I want to play with you chumps or come flying down from the rafters firing the hot dog gun and mooning the crowd at the same time."

"Haven't you done enough flying already?" Travis asked.

Nish answered with his usual response to criticism: a loud raspberry directed Travis's way.

• • •

The Owls would be short a key player for their evening game. It was to be a significant round in the Bell Capital Cup. First, Kazakhstan was up against Slava Shadrin's Moscow team – "New Russian style versus Old Russian style," Muck said, almost rubbing his hands together with anticipation. Following that, the Screech Owls would take on the Vancouver Little Giants.

These two A-level matches were scheduled for the Olympic-size rink at the Sensplex. The winners would then meet each other in the final – with the last game of the tournament scheduled to be played at Scotiabank Place on New Year's Day.

"We've got to make that final," said Fahd. "There will be television there from all over the world."

"First concentrate on getting there," said Travis. "Our job right now is to get by Vancouver." He hoped he sounded like Travis Lindsay, Team Captain, not Travis Lindsay, Old Woman.

"We'll do it," said Lars. "We'll do it."

They headed off early to watch the first game: the Kaz kids against Slava's team. The word had spread about the strange way the Kazakhstan team played, and people wanted to see. Those who weren't coming to see Kazakhstan were out to see Slava, who was, at the age of twelve, already being predicted to be a Number One NHL draft pick six years from now. He was the tournament superstar and the leading scorer so far in the Bell Capital Cup.

The Owls squeezed into a top row of the seats. The big Sensplex rink was sold out, with more fans outside pressing up against the windows that looked onto the big ice surface.

Travis noticed instantly the added passion to the game. It was evident right from the opening faceoff, when one of the larger Kazakhstan players threw his shoulder into Slava before either of them had even tried to get at the puck. The referee let it go.

This was a genuine rivalry, Travis knew. You could almost *smell* it as the two teams felt each other out and began making tentative attacks. It was the most physical game Travis had seen so far, including the ones the Owls had been in, and he couldn't help but think there was something behind the checks other than a desire to take the other player out.

It wasn't just Kazakhstan against Moscow, it was hockey philosophy against hockey philosophy. As Muck had explained, in the years after the 1972 Summit Series, the Soviet teams gradually began modifying their style so it was more like that of the NHL, just as the NHL, even more slowly, began modifying itself to the European game. Kazakhstan, however, remained locked in the old system, which many Russians still believed was superior.

Slava quickly put that into some question, scooting up-ice with the puck, dancing it into his skates as he split the Kaz defence, and sliding a backhander in through the goalie's five-hole. He then put Moscow up 2-0 with a glorious saucer pass to a winger that flew softly over the stick of one defender, over the body of the other, and landed perfectly on the tape of his teammate for an easy shot into the open side.

The Kazakhstan team was down, but far from out. They kept circling back, waiting, waiting, waiting. Finally they spied an opening, and one forward shot through, a pass connecting just as he crossed the Moscow blue line. He was in immediately and roofed a backhander as neatly as Dmitri did himself. A big Kaz defenceman then tied the game just before the final period on a blistering slapshot from the point – a shot so hard and accurate it was worth risking a broken stick.

While the Zamboni was out flooding the ice for the final period, the Owls began moving toward the snack area to get some drinks. But then out of the Zamboni chute came Spartacat, and behind Spartacat, noticeably limping, came a smaller version of Spartacat. Sparta-kitten.

Nish?

Except no one but the Owls knew it was Nish. He had on a smaller version of the mascot's outfit – it looked shorter in the arms and legs – the head the only thing the same size as Spartacat's. After all that news coverage, thought Travis, it was a wonder Nish's mascot head hadn't had to be made even *bigger.* Muck better not see this.

Sparta-kitten was pulling a bag behind him. Spartacat was holding the Master Blaster. They stopped at centre ice, and Nish hauled something wrapped in foil out of the bag and stuffed it down into the Blaster. Spartacat then turned and fired into the crowd. Nish stuffed another in, and Spartacat fired again.

Everyone forgot about the snack stand. The crowd roared its approval, and young peewee hockey players began hurdling seats and lunging for the foil-wrapped projectiles.

Jesse caught one and opened it. It was steaming! *"A hot dog!"* he shouted. *"Thank you, Nish!"*

It was raining hot dogs. As fast as Nish could stuff them into the Master Blaster, Spartacat was firing them into the crowd. Load, click, fire . . . load, click, fire . . . load, click, fire. Travis had to admire the way Spartacat did it so smoothly. It was almost athletic.

Those Owls who didn't catch free hot dogs – and it seemed to Travis that Spartacat had purposely directed extra shots into their row – went off to buy their own snacks and drinks in time for the final period.

The Kazakhstan kids were first back out onto the ice, the Moscow team following shortly after. Both sides had their "game face" on – serious, determined, ready.

Travis looked down the row at Muck. One of Spartacat's hot dogs could have hit Muck on the nose and he wouldn't have noticed, so focused was the Owls' coach on this game. Muck was in his element, studying the action the way someone else might study a math problem or the engine of a car in need of repair.

Slava won the opening faceoff for the Moscow team and circled back into his own end with the puck, drawing two Kaz checkers with him.

He then did something only the inventive Slava Shadrin would dare to attempt. Going almost at full speed toward his own end, with the two checkers racing to catch him, he brought the heel of his stick down hard on the puck and sent it back between his own skates and past both checkers. He then turned so quickly, they both shot by him, one falling as he tried to catch himself and turn.

Slava gobbled up his own "pass," instantly heading up-ice as he led a three-on-two break against the surprised Kazakhstan defence. He cut across the blue line and drifted toward the boards, drawing one defender to him.

Using the boards, he backhanded a sharp pass that bounced off the side and perfectly met the stick of the Moscow winger coming in just behind him. Instantly, Moscow had a two-on-one. The winger passed to the other winger, who shot quickly, and the Kaz goaltender went down, stacking his pads and blocking the shot.

The rebound came straight out to Slava, now skating fast to the net. He chipped the puck into the air so it cleared the sprawling goaltender and then rapped the fluttering puck out of the air like he was bunting it, baseball style, into the net.

"Absolutely *brilliant!*" Sarah screamed as she and the rest of the crowd leapt to their feet to cheer Slava's spectacular play.

Moscow had the lead. But Kazakhstan seemed not the slightest bit fazed by the quick goal. The Kaz kids worked the puck into the Moscow end and began cycling it in a way that made Travis think he was seeing things.

All three forwards skated into the same corner, the first one picking the puck off the boards and then dropping it for the next forward, swooping in just behind. The second dropped to the third, the third dropped to one of the defence pinching in and joining the cycle. As each Kaz player dropped the puck, he deftly took out each Moscow player trying to break the cycle. A little shoulder tick here, a quick hip check there, or perhaps just ploughing into the checker as if he hadn't seen him. The referee, convinced he was seeing accidental contact, let the play go on.

Finally, the Kazakhstan defence dropped to the first forward, who found a seam in the Moscow defence and burst through it, deking the goaltender once before sending a wraparound pass back across the crease to a teammate who one-timed it into the empty net.

"*Awesome!*" screamed Travis as he jumped to his feet with the rest of the Owls.

He looked down the row. Muck was still sitting, but he was grinning from one side of his face to the other and nodding his head up and down furiously. It was, Travis well knew, Muck's equivalent of leaping to his feet and pumping both fists in the air.

The Kazakhstan team seemed to find inspiration from the cycling play, and from that point on they owned the puck. They stickhandled as if the puck were attached by tape to their sticks. They dropped the puck into areas where no player was, only to have a Kaz player instantly appear there and grab it for another circling wave in search of a break to the Moscow net.

They went ahead 4–3, then 5–3, then scored an empty-net goal on the frustrated, exhausted Moscow team to win their division and advance to the finals.

Travis was torn. He hated to see his friend Slava lose, yet he so badly wanted to play against this extraordinary team himself.

Kazakhstan was already in the finals. But the Owls still had to get there.

THERE WAS AN HOUR'S BREAK BETWEEN THE
two division finals. Sarah and Travis went off to the
Moscow dressing room, where they tried to comfort
a tearful Slava. But there was little they could do.
Slava would deal with his disappointment in his own
way, even if it meant weeping openly as he packed
away his equipment. Travis had never known anyone
as competitive as this young Russian. No wonder
everyone believed such a big future awaited him.

"Let's find Nish," Sarah suggested.

As they walked along the hallway, the Zamboni
driver drove in off the ice, and Travis yelled up to
him that they were trying to find the mascots. The
man pointed to the far end of the Sensplex rink,
where there were extra dressing rooms.

"Number 6," the man yelled down.

"Thanks," Travis said, and he and Sarah hurried
to find it.

They knocked.

"C'mon in!" a cheery voice yelled.

They found Nish and Rudy sitting in identical poses, mascot heads off and placed to the side, Spartacat bodies still on, bottles of cold Gatorade in hand, and sweat pouring off them both.

Travis had rarely seen Nish look so content.

"Muck won't like it," Sarah said straight away.

"Muck doesn't know," Nish said. "And what he doesn't know can't hurt him." He winked at Rudy.

"He'll have noticed the limp," Travis said.

Nish looked doubtful. "Muck watch the between-period entertainment? I don't *think* so. He'd be off in his dream world."

Travis knew he was probably right. Unless it was hockey or history, Muck didn't seem to notice much that was going on. He didn't dress like other coaches – Muck preferred his old team jackets to fancy suits – and he didn't have the slightest interest in shopping or souvenirs or watching television. He read, and when he wasn't reading he was planning hockey strategy.

Rudy offered Travis and Sarah drinks of Gatorade, but they said they shouldn't. They were on the ice in half an hour.

"Sit down, then," Rudy said with a smile. "Save your legs for the game."

Travis noticed that Nish did everything exactly as Rudy did it. If Rudy took a slug of his drink, Nish took a slug. If Rudy wiped the sweat off his forehead with a towel, Nish wiped the sweat off his forehead with a towel.

John was also there, but he was busy in the corner with the Master Blaster and hadn't even seemed to notice the two coming in. He cursed mildly as he clicked on something.

"Try holding it in your other hand," Rudy yelled over. "It's easier."

John switched the gun over to his left hand and tried to work the loading and cocking mechanism with his right. He fumbled and almost dropped it.

"I'm left-handed," he said, his face red with what Travis took to be embarrassment.

"Ahhh," said Rudy. "I don't know if they have them for left-handers. There's a catalogue back at Scotiabank Place. I'll check when we get back. If they do, I'll order one for you."

"I'll take this and try it anyway," said John.

Rudy nodded. "Spartacat Number Two," he said, smiling toward John, "is going to have his first outing tonight in the Ottawa Citizen Arena. It's a smaller rink than this one, and it will give him a chance to practice. I'll be there in street clothes, watching."

"Won't people wonder why you're in street clothes?" Travis asked.

Rudy laughed. "No one *knows* me in street clothes," he said. "They don't know me at all if I don't have this on." He patted the Spartacat head beside him.

Travis felt the blood rush to his face. How could he be so stupid?

John was busy loading up a bag with tightly bundled T-shirts to shoot from the Master Blaster. He seemed keen to get going – anxious, Travis figured, to see if he could work the Blaster even though it was made for right-handers.

"We should go," Sarah said. "Mr. Dillinger will be looking for us."

Travis nodded and got up to go, grateful for the opportunity to take his embarrassment with him.

"Good luck tonight," Rudy said. "I'll be cheering for the Screech Owls to reach the finals."

"They're without their top player," Nish said, a self-satisfied grin spreading over his sweaty face.

"What?" Sarah shot back. "Our best player's a *kitten?*"

Sarah and Travis, both giggling, were out the door before Nish could even think of anything to say back to them.

December 29

i have the tool i need in my
hands. it will work brilliantly.

The timing is perfect. The
stage is set for the greatest
performance of my life.
How unfortunate (think of
me as smiling wickedly here)
that those in attendance
will never see another.
Not another performance.
Not another day.

Some of them will be so-called
"innocents." Many of them
will be children. So be it. They
are not innocent, they are the
future of a world that must
have no future. There can

be no turning back. i have
my instructions.

Aha, you say. "instructions"
would suggest this madman — or
is it madwoman? — is under the
control of an outside force.
Perhaps. But who? Or what? is
it another government? Maybe.
Maybe not.

All i can assure you is that
nothing will ever be the same
after i step out onto my chosen
stage for 7/7 and put in motion
the forces that will bring an end
to the madness.

You think i am mad? i think you
are mad. History will prove me
the only sane one present there
that day. Mark my words.

There is little now to do. i
have the tool i need. i have
the setting i am in, and no
one can stop me.

i just have one small annoyance
to deal with.

A bug on my windshield.

Something that needs, and
deserves, squashing.

14

"OKAY!" MR. DILLINGER SHOUTED INTO THE chaos of the Screech Owls' dressing room. "*Listen up! Your coach wants to talk to you!*"

Travis was just pulling on his jersey. He gave the "C" a quick kiss and pulled it down into its position over his heart. He allowed himself a quick giggle at Mr. Dillinger's usual anxiety before a game. Mr. Dillinger got wound up more than any of the kids. His face got flushed. His wispy hair was swept all at odd angles from running his hands through it. He smelt oily and metallic from spending hours bent over the portable skate-sharpening machine. And more often than not he had some smear on his forehead from rubbing it so much. It might be grease or oil from the machine, or it might be from the black hockey tape he was forever fiddling with as he marked time until the game.

There was never any need for Mr. Dillinger to shout "*Listen up!*" If Muck had anything to say, he would say it in such a quiet, calm voice that the kids had to be silent so they could hear. Sometimes, of course, Muck said absolutely nothing. And that, Travis often thought, was when Muck managed to say the most.

Muck came in carrying the game sheet, which he had just finished filling out. He set it down on the tape table and walked over to Travis.

"Stand up, son," he said.

Travis, baffled, stood up.

Muck leaned down and lifted the seat. He read out the words slowly: "Wayne Gretzky sat in this stall during his final game in Canada, April 15, 1999." Muck stood back so everyone could see, though of course everyone already knew by heart what had been written there. *What was he up to?*

Muck took a breath. "That says everything I need to say, kids. Wayne Gretzky . . . Canada . . . A seat of honour. I know you'll play your best tonight – when have the Screech Owls ever failed to do that? – but I also want you to consider something else.

"You have a chance at playing a team that plays a kind of hockey you might never see again. The old Soviet style is as close to ballet as you'll ever come –"

"Yuck!" Fahd whispered. "Ballet sucks."

Muck turned and stared at Fahd. He wasn't angry. "Then think of opera. Or poetry. Or great paintings.

Or classical music. I don't care what you call it, or what some of you even think of it. It's *art*. You win this game tonight, and you go on to play world-class experts of a vanishing art.

"They might not beat you, but they *will* teach you something. And I promise you this: you will never, ever, in your entire lives, forget the experience."

Travis shook his head. He had never heard such a long speech from Muck. Had Muck been drinking? Not possible: Muck's idea of a strong drink was regular Coke.

Muck was just being Muck. He had seen something he thought the Screech Owls should know and appreciate. It didn't matter whether it had anything at all to do with hockey. Muck, after all, was the sort of coach who would order Mr. Dillinger to pull the bus over in the dead of winter so all the players could file outside to read a plaque about some map-making instrument that had been lost hundreds of years ago.

The Owls were still giggling over that one.

"Have fun tonight," Muck said.

He was finished talking.

● ● ●

The Vancouver Little Giants were impressive in the warm-up and doubly impressive once play began.

They were big, much bigger than the Owls, and fast and physical. They were also well coached: A man in a fancy suit with his hair slicked back stood behind the bench, with two other men in suits and slicked-back hair standing on either side of him. Also behind the bench were two equipment managers and a trainer, all in matching track suits.

The Screech Owls had Muck in his old windbreaker and Mr. Dillinger, in a dull-grey track suit, setting up the sticks and the water bottles and, if necessary, prepared to go out onto the ice to apply first aid to an injured player.

Travis's line started, still without Nish on defence. Wilson was there with Fahd, and Sam would be double-shifted at times, but Nish would be missed. Travis would have to pay extra attention to backchecking. No problem, he figured. With his speed, and the speed of Dmitri and Sarah, the Owls top line could get back in time if necessary. The other lines he wasn't so sure of.

Sarah took a hard hit off the faceoff and went down. The whistle blew down the play but signalled no penalty. The referee merely wanted to make sure Sarah was all right. Dmitri slammed his stick in protest and the ref immediately turned, blew his whistle again, and sent Dmitri off for unsportsmanlike conduct.

Travis had to bite his tongue not to protest himself. The Owls didn't need to be two men short.

Sarah, badly winded by the hit, went off, and big Andy Higgins came on to take centre, with Sam replacing Wilson back on defence.

Travis looked at the clock. Thirty seconds into the game and already they badly needed Nish.

But the Owls held, thanks to some outstanding goaltending by Jenny. She was in her "zone," as she liked to call it. Travis couldn't see her face, but he didn't need to. He could see her eyes behind her mask. Like lasers.

Late in the penalty kill, little Simon Milliken picked up a loose puck from a rebound Jenny had kicked out and blindly backhanded a high hoist down the ice. It landed just as Dmitri stepped out of the penalty box.

No one could catch him. Dmitri flew in over the blue line, deked, backhanded, and the water bottle flew into the glass.

Screech Owls 1, Little Giants 0.

Vancouver tied the game late in the first and went ahead in the second on a power-play blast from the point that went in off Lars's foot. Lars blamed himself and seemed near tears as he skated off, gingerly dragging the foot that had taken the shot. But it hadn't been his fault. Pucks hit things. They take unexpected bounces. Stuff happens.

Halfway through the third, with the Owls still down by a goal, Jesse Highboy did something no Owl had seen him do before. He *dangled* with the puck. Of all the players on the Owls, Jesse was least likely to hang on to a puck. He was always quick to headman it to the player ahead, always ready to play give-and-go whenever anyone passed to him. It sometimes seemed like Jesse was happier without the puck than with it. But this time he picked it up in his own end, and when he tried to fire a quick pass out to Andy, he whiffed on the pass, his stick passing right over the puck.

It fooled the player coming in to check Jesse and he flew right by, into the Owls' corner.

Jesse forgot about his missed pass and started carrying the puck. It seemed he was moving in slow motion. Andy circled back and called for another pass by slamming his stick on the ice, and this time Jesse deliberately faked a pass and held, throwing off another checker. He moved over centre and to the blue line, a big Vancouver defenceman coming hard at him.

"Dish it off!" Travis called from the bench. He'd seen Lars rushing to join the play, and all Jesse had to do was flick it across and Lars could pick it up. But instead Jesse did a deft little "tuck," using the curl of his blade to cradle the puck and bring it in tight to his skates.

The defenceman played the puck – "Never play the puck, play the man," Muck always preached to his defence – and in doing so completely miscalculated. Jesse was in alone.

"*Move it!*" Sarah called out from the bench.

It was as if they were watching a replay with the speed slowed down so the announcers could tell exactly what was happening. But this was real time, and Jesse, moving like an old dog, simply wandered in, pulled the goalie out and down, and fired a forehand shot high into the far corner.

"*Mario Lemieux!*" Wilson screamed from the bench, laughing.

The Owls were all laughing – even Jesse. He skated over for his high-fives and fist bumps. He had just scored the best goal of his life playing a style no one had ever imagined him capable of playing.

Jesse came to the bench and sat down, his back still being slapped by his teammates and his face red with excitement.

Muck leaned over and with a big hand tweaked the back of Jesse's neck.

"Next time, pass," Muck said. Jesse looked up, but it was obvious from Muck's wink that he was delighted with what Jesse had just done.

The clock entered the final two minutes – stop time – and Muck decided to go all out in the time remaining. He put Sarah's line out and Sam and

Fahd on defence. He would have preferred Sam and Nish. But Fahd had played a solid game and was enough of a stay-at-home defenceman that he would protect Sam if she decided to rush.

Vancouver won the faceoff and chipped the puck down the ice. Fahd was already back to pick it up.

Travis felt his legs come back completely. In fact, he felt nothing – but that meant he was back to imagining his skates were a part of his own body. He wasn't even thinking; he was just doing.

Fahd fed Travis the puck and Travis instantly felt the presence of rushing Vancouver forecheckers. They were trying to press him, hoping to force him to cough up the puck.

He had two men on him. Sam was expecting a cross-ice pass, but it would have to be on Travis's backhand. He wasn't willing to risk a backhand on the off-curve of the stick – a shot that sometimes can go flat. He remembered Slava's great move against the Kazakhstan team.

He let the puck drift ahead of him, then brought the heel of his stick down hard on it. The puck shot back between Travis's skates, splitting the two for-wards, both of them caught off guard. Travis stopped instantly – "stopped so hard on a dime," Muck liked to say, "that he left a nickel's change" – and reversed direction.

He shot out of his own end with the two fore-checkers well behind, now giving frantic chase. Travis fired a long pass clear across the Olympic-size ice surface to Dmitri, who knocked it down with his glove and onto the curved blade of his stick.

Dmitri cut for the middle, carrying the puck beautifully, and began sweeping around the far defenceman. He kept going, but he left the puck for Sarah, who read the play perfectly, kicking the puck up to her stick as she crossed the Vancouver blue line.

Sarah flew in along the side and faked a slapshot, sending the one remaining defenceman down in a vain attempt to block a shot that never came. The defenceman slid harmlessly toward the boards.

Sarah shifted on her skates so she was gliding side-ways and hit Travis with a pass as he charged in hard along the far side. He took the puck, set, and drove every ounce of his little body into the shot.

The drive clanged off the far post.

Then clanged off the near post.

And in!

Travis hit the ice, spinning like a wheel into the corner. The Owls pounded down on him, Sarah first to land.

Travis had only one thought. How much time was left?

He peeked out through the mass of arms and legs.

Five seconds.

Not enough for Vancouver. Just right for the Screech Owls.

They were in the final!

IT WAS SUPPOSED TO BE A HOCKEY TOURNA-ment, but on this morning the Bell Capital Cup felt more like a set for a Hollywood action thriller.

It was New Year's Day, the first day of the first month of the new year, and the roads around Scotiabank Place were empty but for the police cars with their flashing lights and the endless hum of low-flying helicopters overhead.

The Screech Owls had come early to the big rink to sit and think and get ready for the championship game, which would be played at noon. It was a good thing they came early, as it took Mr. Dillinger more than an hour to crawl from the Queensway into the lower parking area near the back of the rink, where players and officials had been told to enter.

They were intercepted on the ramp heading into the parking area and ordered to pull over. While a security force checked out the bus's luggage storage area, the engine, and even examined the under-carriage with mirrors attached to long handles, three police officers, one of them with a dog, came onto the bus. They checked every player's name against a list on a clipboard and demanded photo ID from both Muck and Mr. Dillinger.

The policeman with the dog walked it slowly up the aisle, letting it sniff under the seats and in various backpacks the kids were carrying.

"You better keep that dog away from Nish's equipment bag," Sam joked to the cop. "It'll ruin him for life."

The policeman never even cracked a smile. Sam went quiet and red at the same time. No one else said anything.

Travis could not believe how serious and how thorough they were. When he thought about it, he knew why. The most powerful men and women in the world were coming here for this one peewee hockey game. The president of the United States and the prime minister of Canada and the president of Mexico were all coming. The prime minister of Britain, the president of France, the president of Russia, and the leaders of a dozen other countries would be in attendance.

Not only that, but the diplomatic community of Ottawa, the nation's capital, was also joining in the celebration of youth and physical activity. Dozens of ambassadors and consuls and diplomats were going to be seated in corporate boxes around the rink.

The *Ottawa Citizen* was calling it "the biggest assembly ever of world leaders." Television crews that had come from around the world to cover the economic summit were on their way to the rink.

This *was* serious, Travis thought. The cop who missed any little sign that things were not right was in danger of putting the most important people in the world in peril.

The dog had reached Nish, who was holding down his usual seat in the back of the bus. The dog sniffed and sat down and whined, staring hard at Nish.

"*What?*" Nish said, more to the dog than to the policeman.

"What's under your jacket?" the policeman asked sharply.

"Nothin'."

"Don't play games, son. What do you have there?"

The other two police officers were now standing directly behind the dog handler. They both had their hands on their gun holsters, ready.

Nish was sweating – an amazing feat in the back of a near-heaterless bus in the dead of winter.

"Very slowly, son, pull out your hands," the policeman ordered.

Nish winced. His face was scrunched tight as a fist, red as a goal light. Slowly he pulled out his hand

and opened it. He was holding the biggest handful of green licorice Travis had ever seen.

The policeman smiled, finally. "Sentinel *loves* green licorice. How did you know?"

Nish was too rattled to answer properly. "I dunno – lucky, I guess."

"Well," the policeman said, "are you going to share?"

His hands shaking badly, Nish peeled off a string and handed it over. Sentinel vacuumed it down so quickly it disappeared quick as a lizard's tongue.

"Just one?" the policeman said.

Nish peeled off another. *Slurp* – it was gone.

"Good luck, boys and girls," the policeman said as he stepped away, pulling on a dog that was now trying to lick Nish's face.

"Do your country proud."

• • •

There were more checks at the entrance to the arena. Men wearing surgical gloves went through each hockey bag, piece by piece. The kids then had to dump their pockets and walk through a metal detector while their bags journeyed down a conveyor belt and through an X-ray machine.

Finally they were in.

"You good to play?" Travis asked Nish as they dropped their bags.

"I'm always good to play – today I'm *great* to play."

"Okay," Travis said. "You take the Gretzky seat."

Nish was almost speechless. "What?"

"Go ahead – maybe it'll inspire you."

"But you –"

"It's all right. I cleared it with Muck and Mr. D. You can sit there for the final, since you're going to try and play."

Nish's eyelids batted up and down as if he were trying to make his eyes talk instead of his mouth. He couldn't say a word. Finally, he nodded, kicked his stinking equipment bag over in front of the Gretzky seat, and sat down as if he had just found the throne from which he would rule for the rest of his life.

"We don't like what we see after the first period, you're out of that seat," kidded Sam.

Nish returned to form with a loud, wet, slobbery raspberry.

There was no need to dress for a while. They were still more than two hours early, and Travis, if he needed to, could get into his hockey equipment faster than he could dress for school. Mr. Lindsay sometimes used his wristwatch to see how quickly Travis could dress for hockey. His "personal best" was one minute and forty-seven seconds. That, Travis thought, deserved to be in *The Guinness Book of World Records.*

Nish was icing his knee before the game, so Travis and Sam and Sarah set out to explore the rink. Only they didn't get too far. The most they were allowed to do was stand at the home-team bench and stare. They couldn't go anywhere else. The rest of the big rink was cordoned off by uniformed guards. At each entrance stood a man in a dark suit. The way each one chewed gum with his front teeth and had a small twisting cord leading from his left ear and down into his collar were dead giveaways that he was working undercover.

There were police with dogs checking under every single seat – more than twenty thousand of them. There were police with strange gadgets – one looked like a vacuum cleaner that wasn't quite touching the floor – walking about the corridors, checking the gauges on the machines every so often.

Travis looked up. There were men and women in dark clothing on the steel rafters overlooking the rink. It was difficult to tell from that distance, but Travis thought they were carrying rifles.

Suddenly, this didn't feel much like a hockey game. Travis thought it was sad that important leaders couldn't just go to a hockey game whenever they felt like it.

"Let's go get dressed," Sam said.

Sarah nodded. They needed to get their minds on hockey, and this place — even if it was a hockey rink — was no place to do that.

January 1

Today it happens. Welcome to
the first day of the first month
of the New Year. 1/1 — the Day
of Destiny.

i could not possibly be more
ready. i have placed myself
exactly where i need to be. i have
earned the trust i needed to earn.
— such fools these Canadians
are — and i have only to show up
for it to begin.

i did not even have to deal with
my annoying little problem. in fact,
the problem solved itself. it is
almost as if pure luck follows
me wherever i go. This child was
getting in my way, but events have
now taken him out of my way. He

will still be there, but he will not be
anywhere near me.

He will, it turns out, be directly
involved in the event. He could
not be in a worse place for what
will happen. So be it. My good
luck, his bad.

i will have to move quickly. i
have one matter to deal with, but
that is the simplest matter of all.
i need to remove the one who
opened the way for me. it will
happen with ease. He trusts me
completely. He will require my
assistance this morning, and i
will provide it, but i will also
have chloroform in a cloth in
my hand. There will be no sound,
just silence, for as long as i
need him to be silent.

He is the lucky one. He will
be placed in perhaps the
only location in the building
completely out of harm's way.
My way of saying thanks for
his stupidity.

This is the last you will hear
from me.

But not, i assure you, the last
you will hear of me.

Al

(a.k.a. Your Worst Nightmare)

TRAVIS LINDSAY FELT LIKE HE HAD BEEN plugged into an electric socket. It was as if wave after wave of pure energy was pulsing through his body.

And yet all he was doing was standing at attention for "*O Canada*."

So many times he had chuckled at NHL players as they stood for the anthems, at how some of them seemed to shift from skate to skate in time with the music, how some liked to stutter their skates in the same way, how some half sang along while others seemed completely deaf to the music. Sometimes an entire bench was swaying to some inner rhythm.

Now he understood. He could not be still. He could not think of anything other than the moment that puck would drop. But it seemed to be taking forever.

First, there were introductions of the various heads of government in attendance — a mixture of cheers and boos for both the Canadian and

American leaders, cheers for everyone else – and introductions of the players for the Kazakhstan Komets and the Screech Owls, introductions even of the coaches and training staff, Mr. Dillinger saluting the crowd, Muck totally oblivious to everything around him but for the game about to be played. Then came the anthems. Next would come the faceoff.

Travis couldn't stop shifting impatiently from one skate to the other. He looked to his side and saw that Sarah was doing exactly the same thing. So, too, was Sam. The Owls were going with their top five – Sarah, Travis, Dmitri, Nish, and Sam – and the Kaz team was simply sending out a line. There seemed no difference between their first line and their third or fourth line.

Jeremy was getting the start in goal. He was moving even before the anthems had finished, skating low into his net, shouldering each post, tapping his crossbar, turning quick and ready to play.

The referee checked the goal lights, spread his legs, and dropped the puck hard.

The crowd exploded with a roar.

The final game was on.

Muck was right – this was an experience unlike any the Owls had ever known. It was not just the enormous crowd – responding to every shift in play with what felt like a thunderclap of emotion in the enclosed arena – but what was happening on the ice, as well. The Kaz team was lightning quick, and the players seemed mentally connected to each other, each acutely aware of where the other four skaters were at all times. They never threw a bad pass. They never missed a good one.

It seemed as if the Kazakhstan players had no positions. They lined up as two defence, a centre, a left-winger, a right-winger, but they played as if all five were interchangeable, the right-winger easily dropping back to take the left defence's spot while the defence carried the puck straight up-ice like a centre.

The crowd seemed as entranced as the Owls by the way the Kaz team was playing. It was almost, at times, as if the crowd had somehow grown into one great giant, rumbling a murmur of confusion as a play it hadn't seen before unfolded, a gasp of surprise at a sudden shift, a gigantic sigh of relief when the Owls managed a good check or a save.

Travis knew the Owls would have their hands full. They were already falling back into trap position, sending only one forward in, usually Dmitri, and waiting for the Kaz players to skate out with the puck. If Dmitri could force an early pass, the Owls might pick one off. But it wasn't happening.

Sarah stole a puck at centre with a poke check. The crowd-giant thundered its approval. She picked up the puck and whipped a hard pass to Dmitri, who knocked it out of the air with his knee and caught the puck on the blade of his stick. Travis heard one of the Kaz players shout in amazement. How amazed would he be, Travis thought, if he knew the quick Owl right-winger was also Russian?

Dmitri headed for the corner, stopping, working the boards, looking for an out. Nish was barrelling in from centre. Dmitri sent a quick saucer pass that seemed to land in the middle of nowhere, but Nish knew where it was and was already in full swing.

He hammered into the puck as hard as he could.

The puck flew fast and high and clipped in just under the Kaz crossbar.

This time, the giant exploded. Travis's head was so filled with sound he thought it would burst.

Owls 1, Komets 0.

Travis landed on Nish as the big defenceman spun into the corner. He thought he heard a small cry from his friend. Sarah caught the pile and was screaming over the incredible cheering of the huge crowd. *"A bullet! A real bullet, Nish!"* Nish was back where he should be. The Owls were whole again.

Travis noticed Nish limping as they came off. "Your knee?" he asked.

"I'm fine."

But he didn't look fine. Nish was definitely limping and his face was even redder than usual. Had he hurt his knee again taking that hard shot? Or was it when Travis had jumped on his teammate to celebrate the goal? It didn't much matter how. The only thing that mattered was that Nish was still hurt.

The Kazakhstan team took control of the puck for much of the rest of the opening period. Nish played but kept coming off early. He was crouching down, in obvious pain. Travis noticed Muck signal to Mr. Dillinger to check up on their star defenceman. Mr. Dillinger went over to Nish and began talking, but all Travis could see was Nish's head shaking no, violently. He was going to keep playing.

Travis had a chance late in the period but nicked the post. Sarah missed when she bobbled a breakaway, the crowd groaning as one. Little Simon Milliken almost scored on a tip.

The Kaz team seemed content to play with the puck and hold back. Their control was amazing. Travis had never seen such pure skill so close up. Their skating and puck handling was as good as any he'd seen in a peewee player, let alone a whole team of such players. But they weren't attacking. They were waiting.

"Soccer," Muck said at one break. "You bide your time. You wait and see. And then you strike. Be ready for it."

It happened just before the end of the period. The Kaz kids had the puck in the neutral zone and kept sending sideways and even backwards passes to each other, endlessly circling back until it looked as if the

Owls were a concrete dam in a river and the Kaz players were fish that couldn't get past.

Travis decided to chase a Kaz player out of sheer frustration, and the Kazakhstan response came so fast it took Travis some time to realize he'd been the cause of it. The moment he stabbed at the puck carrier and gave chase, the Kaz players had the opening they needed. The sideways passing became forward passing, and in three quick passes a shifty Kaz forward was in on Jeremy and the puck was behind the Owls goalie.

Tie game.

The crowd roared as loud for the Kaz goal as it had for the Owls.' This was no longer the Canadian team against the Old Russians. This was a spectacular hockey game, and the crowd was smart enough to realize they were witnessing something extraordinary.

Nish was limping badly when they went into the dressing room. He sat in the Gretzky seat but seemed unaware of anything but the pain.

"Let me see," Mr. Dillinger ordered.

Nish shook his head. Travis noticed there was more than the usual sweat covering Nish's face. Tears were rolling down his chubby cheeks.

"Now!" Mr. Dillinger commanded. It was so unusual for him to speak sharply that Nish immediately stepped up and took off his jersey. He

unstrapped his pants, dropped them, and then unbuckled his right sock and very gingerly peeled it off over the shin pad. When the loosened shin pad fell away, it revealed a knee swollen to twice its normal size.

"You're out of the game," Mr. Dillinger said.

"But –"

"No arguing," Muck said from behind Mr. Dillinger. He was looking down at the knee with concern. "You played a great period. But you can't go on any more. Get undressed. . . . And Mr. D – get some ice for this lad."

Muck leaned over and quickly ruffled his big hand through Nish's thick, wet hair. It was his way of showing how proud he was of Nish's effort. He said nothing, but with the simple gesture he told Nish all that needed to be said.

Nish finished undressing. He was in tears. No one thought the worse of him for crying. They would all have done the same. Nish had played magnificently. He had scored their only goal. And he had insisted he could keep playing when it was obvious to everyone that he couldn't.

Travis would never understand his friend. Nish could be the stupidest, most selfish, most rude person in the world one day, and next day he was the ultimate team player, the one player everyone looked to when the going got tough.

Mr. Dillinger brought ice packed in a plastic bag and Nish pressed it tight to his knee. He got up and tried walking.

"You're not playing," Mr. Dillinger said, "so get it out of your mind."

"Just trying to walk," Nish said through gritted teeth. "I'm going to go find Sparty and watch the game with him."

"Sounds good," said Mr. Dillinger. "Just don't walk around too much."

Nish nodded, not even listening.

The intermission was especially long. CNN was doing a live interview with the president of the United States and the prime minister of Canada together – the interview was being broadcast to the arena crowd on the scoreboard – and everything had to wait until it was over.

Travis was champing at the bit. He wouldn't make the same mistake again. No jabbing for pucks he *thought* he could get. Only pucks he *knew* he could get.

They skated out to yet another enormous roar from the crowd. It was a roar of approval, a roar of appreciation for the game. The referee dropped the puck to a huge explosion of cheers, and the second period was under way. It instantly had more action than the first.

The Kazakhstan team seemed in attack mode

now, almost as if they'd been figuring out the Owls' defence strategy during the first period. They were skating with amazing confidence.

But the Owls were not without their own ideas. Muck had told them he wanted to see more shots on goal – "You can never go wrong by going to the net" – and so some of the big shooters like Gordie and Andy and Wilson and Sam were firing at will whenever they got a chance.

It paid off. Sam took a blast from the point that clipped a Kaz defenceman in the hip. The shot angled down and ticked off Jesse Highboy's toe into the net. Jesse hadn't even seen it happen, but now he was the scoring hero in two straight games.

Kaz got that one back easily with an end-to-end rush by one of the defencemen, a player who buzzed so fast around Fahd that the Screech Owl fell over backwards like a tree that had just been felled by a chainsaw.

The Kazakhstan Komets then went ahead 3–2 on a brilliant three-way tic-tac-toe that left the third player in with nothing but empty net to tap the puck into.

The horn blew. End of the second period.

"I like what I'm seeing."

Muck was doing something very rare. He was talking to the Owls between periods. Not correcting anything, just encouraging them. If Muck liked what he was seeing, so would the crowd.

Travis knew it was already a very good game. Perhaps it would end up being a great game. It might even be the greatest game he had ever played in – no matter which team won the championship.

Muck sent them out early for the third period, again skating out to a roar of approval that suggested the real winners of this remarkable game were those lucky enough to witness it. The Owls arrived in the middle of Spartacat's hot dog Master Blaster act, the crowd screaming even louder, section by section, to get his attention. Spartacat, standing near centre ice, cocked a hand to his ear to get the sections to roar louder. If he liked what he heard, he rewarded them with a foil-wrapped hot dog.

Travis looked for Nish. It wouldn't surprise him if he was somewhere near, perhaps even feeding the hot dogs into the Blaster.

But no Nish. Holding the bag of hot dogs for Spartacat was, as usual, one of the pretty young women.

But Travis noticed something different. Something . . . wrong.

"WHAT IS IT?"

The question came from Sarah. She was shouting into Travis's ear over the roar of the crowd. Sarah had sensed his sudden jolt of surprise as he'd seen Spartacat firing into the crowd.

"*Spartacat's not right!*" Travis shouted, confusion in his voice. He was watching the mascot cock the Master Blaster and shoot. Spartacat had to switch hands to do it, and twice the hot dogs fell from the barrel before he could fire them into the wildly screaming crowd. It wasn't at all smooth, not the way Rudy, the real Spartacat, did it. It had to be John – the backup – the left-hander.

But why, Travis wondered, would Spartacat give up the chance to perform his act before the prime minister and the president and all these heads of government – not to mention all the television networks covering the big event? Even the officials from *The Guinness Book of World Records* were here to confirm this as the world's biggest peewee hockey tournament. This night would go down in history!

Wouldn't Rudy want this show, of all shows, to be as perfect as possible — not a fumbled performance by a mascot-in-training.

"*Look!*" Sarah screamed.

She was pointing up. Travis looked high into the rafters. With the between-period lights on full, he could see that a trap door had opened and a head was sticking out.

It was Nish.

"*Tell me no!*" Sarah shouted. "*He's not doing a moon dive!*"

"*No!*" Travis yelled back over the crowd. "*It's something else!*"

Travis knew his best friend wouldn't actually drop down from the rafters flashing his bare butt at all these government leaders. Something far more important was going on. Nish seemed to be helping someone behind him.

The trap door opened wider. Another head appeared.

Spartacat.

"*Two* Spartacats?" Sarah shouted, her voice totally confused.

People in the crowd had noticed, too. And so had the Spartacat on the ice. He suddenly turned and shoved the young woman who had been stuffing hot dogs into the Blaster. She stumbled and fell hard.

People in the crowd screamed. The security men standing at the exits drew their guns, positioning themselves.

The Spartacat with the Master Blaster reached down into the bag of hot dogs and pulled out something shiny. It wasn't a foil-wrapped hot dog; it was smooth and metallic. He quickly stuffed it down the mouth of the Master Blaster and turned towards the crowd.

The whole crowd was screaming now – much louder than it had ever screamed for hot dogs. They were screaming in alarm and confusion, because the second Spartacat had just dropped through the trap door and was falling, fast, down from the rafters of Scotiabank Place.

The second Spartacat dropped like a stone towards centre ice, straight to where the first Spartacat had taken up his position to fire the hot dogs into the crowd.

The first Spartacat was unaware of anything but the task at hand. He was fumbling with the Master Blaster, desperately trying to get the shiny cylinder down into the tube for firing.

The falling Spartacat hit the standing Spartacat so hard the Blaster flew out of his hands and spun across the ice. The silver canister he had stuffed into the gun bounced away, spinning into the boards.

Guns drawn, the undercover police came running. Two leapt over the penalty box glass and landed on the run, racing toward the two Spartacats. They hit them both at the same time, driving them face-first to the ice as other police surged through the Zamboni chute and onto the ice to assist.

It was impossible, now, to tell the two mascots apart. Both were down on the ice. Both were surrounded by police, their guns ready to fire if necessary.

The heads of government were already being ushered out of the building. The corridors beyond the Zamboni chute were howling with sirens. Travis looked at Sarah. Her eyes were as wide open as her mouth.

Sam ducked in between them. "Want to bet this game is over?" she asked.

NO, NISH HAD MADE NO PLANS TO MOON
twenty thousand hockey fans at Scotiabank Place
and a couple-dozen heads of government – at least
not this time. It was still, he proudly stated, his lifetime ambition to make *The Guinness Book of World
Records* for the largest mass mooning in history. The
world might forget his name, he said. They might
well forget his face. But history, he told them with a
grin, would never forget his butt.

What Nish had done instead was hobble off to
the mascot dressing room. His only plan was to
hook up with his old friend, Spartacat. The original
Spartacat, Rudy – not the fake pretender, John. He
wasn't expected, so he hoped it would be a nice surprise. Nish, after all, had been cleared to play, and as
far as Rudy and John were concerned, Nish was still
dressed for the Screech Owls in the Bell Capital Cup
final against the Kazakhstan Komets.

"I knocked, but no one answered," Nish said. "I figured Rudy was probably out entertaining the crowd, so I went looking for him. Maybe I could even help load the hot dogs for him.

"I found John in the corridor fiddling with the Blaster gun. He had on the second Spartacat suit and didn't even notice me. John's still in training, and it didn't make sense that he was doing the show. So I figured Rudy must be sick or something.

"I went back to the dressing room and found Rudy there all tied up with duct tape."

While Nish freed him from the sticky tape, Rudy tried to make sense of what had happened. He knew John hadn't tied him up just because he wanted to be Spartacat on the big day – it had to be something else.

Rudy had seen John bring in a backpack. He remembered asking John what was in it, just before he smelled the chloroform and passed out. It had to have something to do with the backpack – something John was carrying in it.

There was a television monitor in the mascot dressing room that showed everything the cameras were filming, even when the broadcast switched to commercial breaks. They could see that John was at centre ice entertaining the crowd. Rudy had no idea what exactly was going on, but he knew it was something – and if it had anything to do with the president and the prime minister, he couldn't let it continue.

They knew they'd never get through the security if they just ran out screaming. But Spartacat was free to go anywhere, so Rudy got Nish to help him finish dressing as the mascot. Then they took the freight elevator to the upper bowl and from there climbed a set of stairs that led to a door that took them out onto the rafters. At this point, they were still trying to figure out what John was up to.

It only sank in when they saw John start firing hot dogs with the Master Blaster. Being left handed, he was doing a terrible job of it, fumbling and switching hands, but he also seemed frantic about something.

"When we saw him shove the girl aside and reach for that shiny cylinder thing, we knew we had to act — and there was no time to call anyone. Rudy said if I helped him, he could drop down the wire without John noticing and take out the gun.

"It was the only chance we had — and it worked!"

And so, within the space of four days, Nish had again made the front pages, first as a flying hockey player and now as a hero. He and Rudy were the toast of the town. They had foiled a plot that simply defied imagining. That final "hot dog," it turned out, was an explosive device that would have taken out the entire side of the lower bowl where the heads of government and the ambassadors were sitting.

It would have been devastating, officials said, as bad as 9/11 in New York City or 7/7 in London, England.

It would have been "1/1" – according to a crazed diary that ended up being delivered to the *Ottawa Citizen* two days later.

The small "annoyance" the diarist referred to in later entries, a police analyst said, was none other than Wayne Nishikawa.

The paper ran a picture inside of the two Waynes – Nish standing proudly beside the Wayne Gretzky seat in the visitors' dressing room.

The seat that had almost caused a murder. And the chubby little player from Tamarack who had, almost by accident, ended up preventing many murders.

The organizers of the Bell Capital Cup decided, for the first time in tournament history, to declare two grand champions – the Kazakhstan Komets and the Tamarack Screech Owls. Travis thought it was the perfect outcome. They only played two periods, but it was still the most perfect game the Owls had ever been involved in.

THE END

THE SCREECH OWLS SERIES

1. Mystery at Lake Placid
2. The Night They Stole the Stanley Cup
3. The Screech Owls' Northern Adventure
4. Murder at Hockey Camp
5. Kidnapped in Sweden
6. Terror in Florida
7. The Quebec City Crisis
8. The Screech Owls' Home Loss
9. Nightmare in Nagano
10. Danger in Dinosaur Valley
11. The Ghost of the Stanley Cup
12. The West Coast Murders
13. Sudden Death in New York City
14. Horror on River Road
15. Death Down Under
16. Power Play in Washington
17. The Secret of the Deep Woods
18. Murder at the Winter Games
19. Attack on the Tower of London
20. The Screech Owls' Reunion
21. Peril at the World's Biggest Hockey Tournament

Also available in five omnibus editions!

Ron Devries

Roy MacGregor has been involved in hockey all his life. Growing up in Huntsville, Ontario, he competed for several years against a kid named Bobby Orr, who was playing in nearby Parry Sound. He later returned to the game when he and his family settled in Ottawa, where he worked for the *Ottawa Citizen* and became the Southam National Sports Columnist. He still plays old-timers hockey and was a minor-hockey coach for more than a decade.

Roy MacGregor is the author of several classics in the literature of hockey. *Home Game* (written with Ken Dryden) and *The Home Team* (nominated for the Governor General's Award for Non-fiction) were both No. 1 national bestsellers. He has also written the game's best-known novel, *The Last Season*. His most recent non-fiction hockey book is *A Loonie for Luck*, the true story of the famous good-luck charm that inspired Canada's men and women to win hockey gold at the Salt Lake City Winter Olympics. His other books include *A Life in the Bush, Escape, The Weekender, The Dog and I,* and *Canadians*.

Roy MacGregor is currently a columnist for the *Globe and Mail*. He lives in Kanata, Ontario, with his wife, Ellen. They have four children, Kerry, Christine, Jocelyn, and Gordon.

You can talk to Roy MacGregor at **www.screechowls.com**.